"Not just **my** *daughter, Tate.* **Our** *daughter."*

"Our daughter?" He blinked, uncomprehending. "What are you talking about?"

"When I left here nearly ten years ago, I was carrying your baby."

"A daughter?" Tate felt as if he'd been sucker-punched. "I have a little girl?" He dropped back into the chair and sat there, too shocked to speak.

Taking a deep breath, he thrust a hand over the tips of his hair, sliding the fingers to the back of his head where he held on, trying to keep from losing his mind.

He had a little girl.

A dozen questions crowded his mind.

Why? Why hadn't Julee told him?

And why was she telling him now?

Dear Reader,

Here is an acronym that explains why you should not miss the opportunity to enjoy four new love stories from Silhouette Romance so close to Valentine's Day:

L is for the last title in Silhouette Romance's delightful MARRYING THE BOSS'S DAUGHTER six-book continuity. So far, Emily Winters has thwarted her father's attempts to marry her off. But has Daddy's little girl finally met her matrimonial match? Find out in *One Bachelor To Go* (#1706) by Nicole Burnham.

O is for the ornery cowboy who's in for a life change when he is forced to share his home…and his heart with a gun-toting single mom and her kids, in Patricia Thayer's *Wyatt's Ready-Made Family* (#1707). It's the latest title in Thayer's continuing THE TEXAS BROTHERHOOD miniseries.

V is for the great vibes you'll get from Teresa Southwick's *Flirting With the Boss* (#1708). This is the second title of Southwick's IF WISHES WERE… terrific new miniseries in which three friends' wishes magically come true.

E is for the emotion you'll feel as you read *Saved by the Baby* (#1709) by Linda Goodnight. In this heartwarming story, a desperate young mother's quest to save her daughter's life leads her back to the child's father, her first and only love.

Read all four of these fabulous stories. I guarantee they'll get you in the mood for *l-o-v-e!*

Mavis C. Allen
Associate Senior Editor

Please address questions and book requests to:
Silhouette Reader Service
U.S.: 3010 Walden Ave., P.O. Box 1325, Buffalo, NY 14269
Canadian: P.O. Box 609, Fort Erie, Ont. L2A 5X3

Saved by the Baby

LINDA GOODNIGHT

SILHOUETTE *Romance* ®

Published by Silhouette Books

America's Publisher of Contemporary Romance

This book is dedicated to Samuel Barker.
May you have a long and blessed life. You are my hero.

Special thanks to beautiful fashion model Dani Boatright Hayes, for sharing her
expertise about the modeling industry. To Dr. Travis Goodnight who never grows
impatient with his mother's medical questions. And to two wonderful friends and
fellow writers: Darlene (Graham) Gardenhire and Libby Houghton Banks for
inspiration, insight and the tears that told me I was on the right track.

 SILHOUETTE BOOKS

ISBN 0-373-19709-8

SAVED BY THE BABY

Copyright © 2004 by Linda Goodnight

Visit Silhouette at www.eHarlequin.com

Printed in U.S.A.

Books by Linda Goodnight

Silhouette Romance

LINDA GOODNIGHT

A romantic at heart, Linda Goodnight believes in the traditional values of family and home. Writing books enables her to share her certainty that, with faith and perseverance, love can last forever and happy endings really are possible.

A native of Oklahoma, Linda lives in the country with her husband, Gene, and Mugsy, an adorably obnoxious rat terrier. She and Gene have a blended family of six grown children. An elementary school teacher, she is also a licensed nurse. When time permits, Linda loves to read, watch football and rodeo and indulge in chocolate. She also enjoys taking long, calorie-burning walks in the nearby woods. Readers can write to her at linda@lindagoodnight.com.

Dear Reader,

If ever I wrote a book of my heart, you are holding it in your hands. Immediately after I conceived the idea of a mother's desperate search for a bone marrow donor for her child, my daughter introduced me via e-mail to a family who was fighting the same battle to save their son.

With amazing generosity and sometimes painful honesty, Samuel's family shared his—and their—struggle. They relayed Sam's journey through e-mail updates and heartrending photographs, believing that through the telling, listeners would be moved to give the precious gift of bone marrow so that other children might have a chance at life.

You can't imagine the times I've wept during the writing of this book, knowing that countless real children, like Samuel, fight a daily battle for survival. Nor can you imagine how humbled I am by the faith and courage of Sam and his amazing family. In fiction, I have the ability to be sure everything turns out all right. In real life, this is not always the case. Samuel's recovery has not been easy, but I am thankful to report that at one year post-transplant, he continues to improve.

I hope you are touched and entertained by *Saved by the Baby*. Should you like more information about bone marrow donations visit www.marrow.org or contact your area blood bank.

With best wishes,

Linda Goodnight

Chapter One

"I got five bucks and a bottle of Bud that says she won't stick around two days."

Jeet Hammond lounged a fat elbow on the counter of Harper's Doughnut Shop and pointed his coffee cup at the long-legged brunette sashaying past the picture window. Disinterested, Sheriff Tate McIntyre watched the woman flick in and out of view between the signs plastering the plate glass. He hadn't a clue who his deputy was talking about and he didn't care. Tate had neither the time nor the heart to worry about females.

With a good-natured grin he reminded his deputy of what everyone in the county already knew. "No betting on beer, Jeet. You know I don't drink." Few people understood the reasons why.

"I know, I know, and you don't gamble, either." Jeet's fleshy face wrinkled in mischief. "But I still do."

Tate laughed and pushed back the remains of Clare Harper's almost-famous pecan pie. Then the serendipitous Oklahoma wind teased the woman's shapely legs, lifting the edges of a blue-flowered skirt ever so slightly, and he realized who she was. Suddenly, the pecan pie felt as heavy on his stomach as a watermelon. He hadn't known she was back in town.

Jeet, his head tilted in a comical leer, stared at the billowing skirt and chanted prayerfully, "Higher, higher. Dang, but she has the prettiest legs I ever seen. No wonder them fancy folks out West pay money to take pictures of 'em."

"If your wife heard you talking about beer and some woman's legs at the same time you'd be sleeping in my spare room again."

Jeet had the grace to look guilty, though he continued to follow the brunette's progress until she was out of sight.

"You got that right." He sighed blissfully. "But Tate, old buddy, even a tough case like you has to be affected when Julianna Reynolds shows up in Blackwood after all this time."

Tate shifted uncomfortably and concentrated on his warm, sweet coffee. He was affected all right, but not in the way Jeet had in mind. Ten years ago when Julee had walked away from him on those gorgeous gams she'd taken something he'd never gotten back—his last twenty dollars and a sizable chunk of his heart. He didn't intend that anyone would ever hurt him that way again.

"If she was so successful, how come we never seen no pictures of her?" Jeet craned his head toward the window.

"She's a leg model, Jeet. It's hard to recognize a person by her legs."

He didn't add that he'd recognized Julee every time he'd seen those long perfect legs in a commercial or a magazine. If he thought about it, he could still feel the smooth silk of her skin against his. But he darn sure wasn't going to think about it. Not now. Not ever.

"Some folks said it was her in that movie last year about the ballet dancer."

"Yeah, I heard that."

"Man, that billboard out by the interstate almost made me run off the road the first time I seen it. I bet that was her."

It was Julee, all right. Tate had driven out to that billboard and set up a driver's license check right next to it. Sat up there half the night staring at those legs, writing tickets, and reliving the one memory that haunted him.

A scalding sip of coffee washed down the bitterness that rose every time Tate remembered the woman he'd loved enough to die for. He hadn't been good enough for her. He'd known it then and he knew it now. She deserved a better life, and they'd both known an illegitimate mixed-blood troublemaker from the wrong side of the tracks couldn't give it to her. With an annoyed grunt, he clanged the white mug onto the saucer.

Tossing several bills on the table, Tate rose. "Come on, Jeet. Lunch is over and we've got plenty of work to do."

His portly deputy scraped back from the table, hitched up droopy pants, and followed. "Wonder what she's doing here after all this time."

That's what Tate was wondering, too.

Julianna Reynolds was on a mission.

With a purposeful swing of her famous legs, she strode down the sunny main street toward the Blackwood Municipal Building. With every step nearer the man who held her whole world in his hands, Julianna fretted. He was married, happy, successful. She'd planned never to interfere in the life he'd chosen, but desperate times meant desperate measures. Somehow she'd get his cooperation without ever revealing the real reason for her sudden reappearance in Blackwood. She owed him that much.

The huge clock on the grounds of Evans Funeral Home read a little past noon. She blanched at the grim reminder of death, the terrible vulture hovering over her day and night. Death was her enemy, creeping forward with each passing moment. Only the grace of God and modern technology held the monster at bay for now.

The warm spring breeze stirred the scent of tulips in the brick planters on each side of the tall courthouse steps. Without pausing to admire their beauty, Julianna opened the heavy double doors and entered the cool, dim interior.

Megan, her only child, the light of her life, her reason for living, was dying. Only a bone-marrow transplant could save her, and after several weeks of searching and testing, no donor match had been found. So, Julianna had done what she'd sworn never to do. She'd packed a bag and come back to Blackwood to find Megan's father. She'd come home to find Tate McIntyre.

No one sat at the reception desk outside the wooden door marked Seminole County Sheriff. Julianna paused, gathering courage to open the door. Throat dry as cotton, her confidence waned. What if he refused? What if this plan to save Megan failed? Drawing a deep breath to calm her trembling insides, she turned the knob to Tate's office.

The door was locked. Shoulders sagging in disappointment, she leaned her forehead on the cool brass plate bearing Tate's name. If she hadn't already cried enough tears to fill a football stadium, she'd have broken down.

''Looking for someone?''

At the deep, gravelly voice, Julianna jerked her shoulders back to flawless posture and whipped around. Tate McIntyre, older, bigger, and far more handsome than she remembered stood a mere three feet away.

Her heart did a foolish jitterbug that she chalked up to nerves. She was scared silly, not attracted, though any female alive would notice this tall, dark lawman.

Wearing a shuttered expression above a crisply pressed uniform shirt, creased blue jeans and brown boots, he was still Tate, but with tantalizing changes. Lean and tough looking, he brought to mind a marine. The tall, anvil-shaped body that had made him a top football recruit filled out the sheriff's shirt to perfection, the olive color emphasizing his mocha skin and green eyes. His brown-black hair was shorter, the almost military cut highlighting the high cheekbones of his Native heritage. Julianna's stomach dipped. The handsome boy had become a stunning man. A man who had chosen another woman over her.

From somewhere in the building came the static of a police radio. Tate cocked his head to listen, not taking his eyes off her for a minute.

She'd wondered about him many times over the years, but nothing had prepared her for this moment. Her ears rang and blood pulsed at her temples. Some deeply buried emotion threatened to rear its head as she took in the man she'd once loved with all the teenage passion possible. She fought it back. Tate was the past, and she was here for Megan. Only for Megan.

Suddenly short of breath, Tate stared at the tall, willowy brunette with a death grip on his office doorknob. Julee Reynolds was not only back in town, she was standing outside his office, looking up at him with anxious blue eyes that threatened to undermine his resolve never to get emotionally involved with a woman again.

With steely control, he drew some air into his tortured lungs. She'd always been beautiful to him, even when the other guys had called her "Olive Oyl" and "Toothpick," but years of working in an industry where beauty is carefully cultivated had enhanced her natural assets. He didn't want to notice, didn't want to feel a thing in her presence, but he did.

"Hello, Tate."

She extended a hand—a long, manicured hand with those fancy fake nails women liked. Fool that he was, he wrapped his fingers around hers. The jolt of awareness from her skin to his was as powerful as the stun gun they'd zapped him with in the police academy. She was warm and soft and—criminy, she was Julee, the woman who'd taken his heart to L.A. and never sent it back. That's why he couldn't breathe, couldn't talk. Heck, he couldn't even think.

Like his father, Julee had been relegated to a mental file marked "unsolvable case" so he could move on with his life. Maybe that's why seeing her affected him so strongly and brought back an avalanche of unwanted feelings. Time and hard work had distanced him from most of the pain in his past, but nothing had ever filled the void Julianna had left when she'd stepped on that old Greyhound bus and ridden away.

He'd known she had to give the modeling world a shot, had wanted that for her. She and her mom had already lost their house and were barely holding things together. He just hadn't realized it would hurt so much when she never came back, especially after his career-ending injury. Eventually, pain turned to resentment and resentment to bitterness. She'd proved him right. He wasn't worth her coming back to. He'd fallen into a black hole after she left and nearly destroyed himself. Since then, he'd kept his heart locked away, taking care not to risk that kind of rejection ever again.

If he had a lick of sense, he'd find out what she wanted and send her back to L.A.—ASAP.

"How are you?" Her voice was that smooth honeyed alto that had once sent his teenage libido into overdrive. Just talking to her on the phone had been a sexual fantasy. Sexiest voice, sexiest legs, sweetest girl on the planet.

He slammed the cover on that file so fast his brain ached.

"Doing good. Yourself?" He willed himself to release her hand, then reached around her and unlocked his office so they could go in. Lord knew he needed to sit down and get a grip.

Standing aside, he let her enter first, catching the subtle drift of some designer perfume. He couldn't name it. Never was good at that sort of thing, though he could sniff out a meth lab or a drunk driver with his eyes closed.

"It's been a long time," she said, her blue gaze drifting around the old, narrow office that he'd worked so hard to gain. His desk, always a cluttered mess, looked even more so today. The air-conditioning wheezed and rattled and little dust wads flapped in the vent. To her big-city eyes, accustomed to the best, he supposed this place looked and smelled like a musty hole in the wall.

"A very long time," he repeated, glancing at the calendar on his desk. Nine years, seven months and thirteen days, to be exact. The date she'd left him was a permanent scar on his heart, like a bad tattoo that no amount of surgery could remove. "I heard you did all right for yourself."

"You heard?"

He shrugged, not willing to let her know how he'd scrounged for every drop of information, praying she'd make it big then praying she wouldn't. He'd even fantasized about her coming back, broke and lonely. In his dreams, he'd been the man she needed, the only one who could help her. He'd been a dumb kid then who'd believed in the impossible.

Tate shifted the weight off his bad knee. Weather must be changing for the old injury to act up this much. Or maybe it was the eighteen-hour day he'd spent on duty, half of it on his feet, searching the lake woods for a lost child. But Tate had no complaints. He'd felt like a million bucks when he'd placed the boy in his tearful parents' arms.

He knew his stance had given him away when Julee's gaze came back to him, drifting down his body to rest at his aching knee. Though her attention was purely curious, Tate's body grew warmer than the April weather dictated.

"I never did get a chance to tell you how sorry I was about your knee injury. Does it still bother you?"

So she *had* known. And never even called. Apparently, she hadn't given him another thought once she hit the big city.

"Sometimes," he admitted gruffly. Nearly ten years had passed. Why was she bringing it up now?

Julee touched his arm lightly, but enough that the electric shock of her touch still made his insides quiver. Not just physical wanting, though she had that power, too, but emotional need so intense he wanted to collapse at her glamorous feet. After all this time, he was still a fool.

"I always hated what happened to you."

If she'd cared so much, why hadn't she come home? Why hadn't she been the one to see him through those black days? Why had she left him alone to drown in alcohol and self-pity and to marry the first woman who would tolerate both?

"That was a long time ago." He stepped back from the

subtle lure of her perfume, placing the desk between the two of them. "It all happened a long time ago."

They'd been so young, thinking they could have it all. Julee would be a famous model. He'd play pro football. Then they'd find their way back to each other. Trouble was, her dream came true about the same time his died on the ten-yard line with three minutes to go in the first half of the season opener.

He'd fallen into the black abyss of anger and alcohol, too proud to call her, but furious when she didn't call him. Then Shelly had come along, sweet and sympathetic, willing to tolerate his drunken rages and self-pity. She'd been his anchor during a time when he'd wanted to die. Out of some alcohol-distorted sense of gratitude, and because he needed to believe someone cared, he'd married her after less than a month.

Tate squeezed his eyes shut and blotted out the memories. Too much time had passed to go there now. "So. What brings you back to Blackwood?"

And how soon will you be on the next flight out?

Some emotion stirred behind her beautiful blue eyes. What was it? Nerves? Anxiety?

Squinting in thought, he studied the intense set of her jaw, the shadows above her elegant cheekbones. That's when he knew. Julianna was afraid.

The loose rollers on his chair clattered against the brown tile as he pulled it away from the desk. One hand on the nubby gray backrest, he waited, cop instinct on alert.

What was she afraid of? And what on God's green earth could it have to do with the hometown she'd abandoned years ago? Better question, what did it have to do with him?

"Mind if I sit down?" she asked. Tate tried to ignore

the tingle in his gut whenever her lips moved. "I have some important business to discuss with you."

Fighting the need to protect her from whatever demon chased her, and the greater need to protect himself from her, Tate indicated the green vinyl-covered chair across from his desk, then settled into his own. Immediately, he wished he hadn't. Julee sat, crossing her long beautiful legs directly in his line of vision. His chest tightened. Sitting upright, he steepled his hands beneath his chin to block the view. He had to get her out of this office.

"Business?" Curiosity got the best of him. What kind of business could bring Julianna Reynolds back to Blackwood?

When she leaned forward, expression earnest, her silky blue blouse gapped slightly, affording him an unwanted glance of creamy skin. Infuriatingly, his body reacted. She was sexy, vulnerable and beautiful, a combination that spelled danger for any man but was deadly for him. She was big city and he was small town. She was rich and he was a working stiff. And she was, as her mother had once said, "too good for that McIntyre boy."

Criminy! Why he was thinking this way? He didn't know this woman. Hadn't known her for years. All they had was the past, and that was better left alone.

The phone emitted a soft buzz, and he barely held back a curse. He was too busy to worry over Julianna Reynolds, and the sooner he found out what she wanted, the sooner she'd be gone and he'd be safe from thinking too much.

Holding up one finger of his left hand in a "wait-a-minute" gesture, he punched a button with the right. "Yeah?"

His receptionist's voice came out of the speakerphone. "Mrs. Barkley needs you to drive by her place. She's sure the Peeping Tom is back."

Taking out his annoyance on the receptionist, he growled, "Where have you been?"

"Even Rita the Magnificent has a bladder, Tate. Don't get your tail in a twitch."

He glanced at Julee, saw her struggling with a grin, and was relieved when she rose and starting roaming the room. He swiveled sideways to avoid watching the swish of her blue skirt against silken thighs.

Having Julee in his office was bad enough without the hired help humiliating him. Smart-aleck receptionist. But he knew better than to cross Rita the Magnificent. She was a lot more than a receptionist, and he couldn't manage without her. "Tell Mrs. Barkley I'll be there as quick as I can."

"Oh, she said there's no big hurry. And she wants to know if you'll stop by the store and get Penelope some cat food before you come out."

Tate gave in to a grudging grin. He'd investigated her "Peeping Tom" four times in as many months. Poor old Mrs. Barkley. Anything for a little company. He wondered what kind of cake she'd baked this time and hoped he'd have time to eat a piece of it while she entertained him on the piano.

"No problem."

From the corner of his eye he could see Julee surveying the row of framed certificates and citations hanging around his small, cluttered office. He hoped she wouldn't miss the college diploma. She'd had success handed to her on a silver platter, but he'd worked plenty hard for his.

As he started to disconnect, Rita spoke again. "Don't forget you need to be back in time for Little League practice."

"Anything else?"

"I left the list on your desk. A meeting with the county

commissioner at four, the task force tomorrow morning, Martha's birthday party and the slave auction at the high school—"

"Hold on." He scrounged around in the enormous stack of folders and papers. The list lay in plain sight beneath a snow globe paperweight that Jacob, his seven-year-old buddy from the Big Brother program, had given him last Christmas.

"I found it." He stuck the list in his shirt pocket and shut off the receptionist's disembodied voice.

Julee's blue gaze, wide with curiosity, drifted back to him. "You *are* a busy man."

"Goes with the job. So if you don't mind..." He let the words trail off hoping she'd take the ball and run with it. Her visit was starting to get under his skin.

Before she lost her nerve, Julianna settled back into the green chair and plunged into the story she'd rehearsed for days.

"I've come home to Seminole County to do some charity work. You know. One of those celebrity things that are good for an income tax break."

She blasted him with a hundred-watt smile as fake as the words she'd spoken. She'd never done a "celebrity thing" in her life. Though she'd worked tirelessly to increase bone-marrow donors and had even headed a previous drive, celebrity had nothing to do with it. Outside the modeling industry and this small town she had no celebrity status, but Julianna prayed Tate wouldn't know that. Finding cures for sick children had simply become her passion.

Tate arched an eyebrow. Stacking his hands behind his head, he tilted back in his rather bedraggled roller chair. "What could that possibly have to do with me?"

Julee crossed her arms over her middle. She hadn't expected a red-carpet welcome after all these years, but his cool appraisal turned her butterflies into swarming buzzards.

Behind him, through the window, Julianna vaguely comprehended the ebb and flow of light traffic out on the street. A single horn honked. Car doors slammed. The quiet, unhurried normalcy of everyday life in a small town soothed her.

Normalcy—a condition she could hardly recollect. For a while three years ago, life had almost been normal. They'd been sure Megan had been cured by the chemotherapy treatments.

Then had come the frightening news two months ago that Megan's leukemia cells had reappeared, throwing her into the desperate search for a bone-marrow donor, the only hope of cure now that chemo had failed to permanently destroy the disease. Until now they hadn't even considered this last-ditch, drastic kind of treatment. For the first time Julee had no choice but to involve Tate. Megan was in a second drug-induced remission, but the doctors said it was only a matter of time until the cells began to multiply again. How much time, no one could say.

Not one day since then had they lived a moment without fear. Megan, her beautiful nine-year-old daughter, deserved a normal life, and so did dozens of other children awaiting a bone-marrow transplant.

If she could get Tate to donate blood without him knowing about Megan, everyone would be better off—Megan, Tate and his wife. No wife, however devoted, wanted the shock of discovering her husband had an unknown child by his first love. Plenty of reasons to face Tate's chilly regard.

Leaning her elbows on a pile of official-looking documents Julianna locked eyes with the man who held Megan's fate. The air conditioner thumped to life, but even the cool blast of air couldn't counter the tingle of sweat prickling the back of her neck.

"I'm involved with increasing the number of minority donors for the bone-marrow transplant database. Since my hometown happens to be the tribal capital of the Seminole Indians, I thought this would be a good place to start."

The chair rollers clattered to the floor. Tate frowned at her, puzzled, but clearly intrigued. The chatty clerk at the motel had been telling the truth; Sheriff McIntyre was a sucker for a good cause.

"Bone-marrow donation?"

"People wouldn't necessarily be donating their bone marrow. At first, there's just a blood test and the donor information is put into the data bank. Then if someone needs a transplant, doctors can access the data bank for a suitable match."

"I thought relatives usually donated bone marrow."

Julee's pulse kicked up a notch, the falsely chipper smile tightening. "That's the ideal situation, but sometimes family members don't match." *Like me.*

In a deliberate attempt to calm her fraying nerves, Julee picked up the paperweight from Tate's desk and rolled it between her hands, watching snow drift over the pair of baying hounds. Was it her imagination, or could she still detect the warmth of Tate's skin? Oddly, the thought calmed her.

"Any reason why you're targeting minorities?"

Oh, yes, the most important reason in the world. Their daughter had Tate's Seminole heritage and the genetic types that went with it.

"Minorities have a very limited donor system, so the chances of finding a match are almost nil. And because their population is small, we need all the donors we can get.''

"We?"

She shrugged, but her grip on the paperweight was tight enough to turn her knuckles white. She'd done fine without this man for nearly ten years. She had no desire to disrupt her life or his any more than necessary, but Tate's cooperation could save Megan's life. "I've been working with the bone-marrow registry for a while. Too many kids die who could be saved by somebody if only that someone had his blood type on file.''

Her heart had been broken a dozen times as beautiful children she and Megan had come to know had withered away while waiting for a transplant. Minority children especially lacked hope. Somehow, she had to change that.

"Why come to me? Why not go to the hospital or the Chamber of Commerce?''

"I have. The hospital administrator thinks it's a great opportunity for PR. The bone-marrow people will send a mobile unit, the Saturn Company has signed on to sponsor, and we'll accept regular blood donations, too, to help with expenses.''

He tilted back in his chair again, eyebrows knit in thought. Bright sunlight slanted in through the window behind him and gleamed off his almost-black hair. He picked up a pen and rotated it between his fingers. "Let me ask that again. Why come to me?''

"I'm lining up all the community and civic leaders. The mayor, the school administration, fire chief, etc. Since I'm especially interested in bringing the Seminoles on board, your influence…'' At Tate's thunderous expression, Julee clapped her lips together. She'd thought he was warming to the idea, but now the cold, shuttered expression returned.

"You'll have to go to the BIA or tribal chiefs if you want the Seminoles. Don't expect me to get involved."

Her heart fell. "But I thought—"

"You thought what, Julee? That you could march in here and pretend ten years hadn't passed? That I'd ignore the law-enforcement needs of this county to run around drumming up business for your tax break?"

"No! That's not what I thought at all." Where had she gone wrong? "As I said, you're the sheriff, you have a certain clout that could be used—"

"Used? No thanks. Been there, done that."

Julee squeezed her hands into fists, the long nails digging at her skin. She wanted to scream, to cry, to grab Tate and make him listen. Everything was coming out all wrong.

"That's not what I meant!"

With a loud exhale, Tate held out a palm, peacemaker style. "Look, Julee, I don't mean to be a hard case about this, but there are plenty of others to help with this cause of yours. I really am awfully busy, and given our history, I'd expect to be the last man on earth you'd come to."

Their history was exactly why she had to have his help, but for Megan's sake she dared not tell him that. Resuming perfect posture on the slick vinyl seat even while her insides howled in terror, she struggled for control and a serene façade. Any act of hysteria on her part was bound to make him wonder why he was more important than any other civic leader.

"We were once such good friends, I just thought—"

"Once," he interrupted. "And once was a long time ago, a time I don't care to revisit. Now, if you'll excuse me…" He tossed the pen down and pushed upward from the desk. "I have to see a woman about a Peeping Tom."

"Wait. Please." But Tate was past listening.

Julee watched in dismay as the Sheriff of Seminole County, the man whose very blood she depended upon, grabbed his hat and, as if he couldn't stand to be in her presence another moment, strode out the door.

Chapter Two

"He says he won't help, Mom." Julianna gripped the telephone receiver, trying to keep the panic at bay.

"He has to!" Beverly Reynolds' strident voice pierced the distance from California to the Blackwood Motel.

"I know that, Mother," Julianna cried. Then flopping back onto the standard green-and-brown motel bedspread, she relented. "I'm sorry. I'm just so scared. What if I can't convince him to be tested?" She rubbed at the ache building between her eyebrows. "I don't know what I'll do."

The motel television flickered to a commercial and Julianna saw her own legs hawking a new brand of depilatory cream. She turned away from the inane sight.

"I don't know, either, honey." Regret tinged her mother's words. "If I hadn't lied to everyone, especially Megan, you could come right out and tell Tate the truth."

"I don't want to hurt his family, but if he doesn't agree to donate on his own, I'll have no choice."

"No! Absolutely not. You can't risk it." Julianna held the phone away from her mother's screech. "The doctors have told us a dozen times how important a positive mental state is to Megan's struggling immune system. Her health is too fragile to suddenly discover the father she thought was dead is alive and well in Oklahoma. Who knows what the shock might do to her?'' A tormented sigh came through the phone lines. Julianna envisioned her mother repeatedly pushing short frosted hair behind one ear. "This is all my fault. I never should have started that lie.''

"You did what you thought was best at the time, Mama. I don't blame you for any of this.''

When Julee had discovered her pregnancy and Tate's marriage to another woman, her mom had created a deceased husband to save face in the new city and among new friends and co-workers.

"You were so young and so stubbornly determined not to ruin Tate's chances for a football career. For a while I hated that boy. There you were pregnant, trying to succeed in this crazy modeling business, and wanting to spare the very boy who'd gotten you into trouble. I only meant to protect you and Megan from mean-spirited people.''

"I know, Mama, I know.'' Julianna stared at the black spots on the ceiling tile. She'd relived those days in her mind a thousand times wondering what she could have done differently, and the answer always came out the same. She didn't know.

Her mother hadn't wanted her united with Tate, though she'd bitterly resented Julianna's original plan to keep Tate in the dark. But Julee had feared what would happen if he'd discovered the pregnancy. He would have abandoned the athletic scholarship, his only opportunity to move beyond the horrible poverty and despair of his childhood. He would have gone back to work at the gas station and killed himself trying to care for a wife and a baby. In the end, after she'd reconsidered, he'd already traded her for someone else, so she lived with the lie created to protect them all.

"You never did approve of Tate, but he's different now."

"Different? Honey, Tate McIntyre was always different."

"I mean different in a different way." Julee laughed a little at that, comparing the almost military perfection of the Tate she'd seen today with the long black hair, the wary eyes, and bad attitude of the Tate she'd known ten years ago. "I don't believe for one minute he'd intentionally hurt Megan. The bad-boy reject has become the golden savior and this town thinks he walks on water. From all appearances, he's gentle and kind to everyone. Everyone but me, that is."

"I don't see why he should be angry with you," Beverly sniffed defensively. "It's not your fault he lost the football scholarship. And it sure wasn't your fault he married that Atkins girl while you were still carrying his baby. I'll never forgive him for that."

"Mama, don't go there. Please. I've had such a stressful day." Gripping the phone a little tighter, she twisted the cord around her finger. "How's Megan? Is she there?"

"No, she's at school. Since you told her about having a bone-marrow drive where her daddy's relatives lived, and explained how some of them could possibly match, she's been full of zip."

Julianna said a silent prayer of thanks. As long as Megan remained in remission, they had time to search for a donor. Her chest filled with a familiar mix of joy and pain. Being a mother was the hardest and most wonderful thing she'd ever done.

"Has she gained any weight?"

"In two days? Honey." Her mother's voice brimmed

with sympathy. "Megan is like you. She'll never fatten up too much."

Julee had a vision of Megan's wide, omnipresent smile in a narrow face with Tate's high cheekbones and leaf-green eyes. Her arms hung like twigs from her T-shirt sleeves and she'd been bald so often, she'd taken to wearing a ball cap even when her hair had grown out. Julianna's heart expanded with fierce mother love. Megan was an amazing kid, so full of life and love it seemed impossible that she could be dying.

"I have a meeting with the hospital administrator and the radio-station manager in a while, Mom, so I'd better get moving." She sat up on the end of the bed. "Give Megan my love."

"Try not to worry so much, Julee."

"I won't if you won't." It was an oft-repeated phrase.

"Everything is just dandy from this end. Eugene is coming over for dinner and afterward Megan and I have a hot game of Super Nintendo to finish."

Julianna knew her mother and their affable accountant, Eugene Richmond, would be much more than friends if not for her and Megan. She had halfheartedly encouraged the pair to take their relationship further, but in truth, she couldn't work the insane modeling schedules without her mom to help care for Megan. And with Megan's hospital bills, every penny counted. When she'd discovered Julee's pregnancy ten years ago, Beverly had moved to L.A. and become housekeeper and nanny while Julianna had provided the finances. So, adding to Julianna's burden of responsibility, dear Eugene offered only friendship to the woman he wanted to love.

Replacing the receiver, she lay back on the full-size bed. Out of long habit she began the tedious exercises that kept her legs in high demand in commercials, magazine ads and movies. Sometimes, when she wasn't worrying about Megan, she wondered what would happen when her legs gave out. How would she support her sick child? The agency loved her now because of the huge commission she brought in, but she had no illusions about this silly, shallow business of making a living with her body. She was a piece of meat. When the meat turned bad, she'd be nothing.

For the millionth time she wished she'd gotten an education, wished she'd chosen a career that made a difference in life, wished she'd been a nurse or a teacher or something that mattered. Viciously, she bicycled the air. She was nothing, nothing, nothing, but a pair of legs.

Chapter Three

"Crown me."

Tate groaned and gave up one of his checkers, clunking the piece down with feigned annoyance. "You're cheating again, old-timer," he said with affection to the man sitting across from him.

Every Tuesday at noon, rain or shine, Tate attended a Chamber of Commerce meeting in the conference room of Blackwood Community Center, then moseyed over to the Senior Room for a game of checkers or dominoes. Today former sheriff Bert Atkins, his friend and mentor, was beating the pants off him.

"Ha! Don't need to cheat when you play this bad." The older man chortled happily and popped another peppermint in his mouth—his crutch to avoid smoking. "You must be working on a case the way your mind is off somewhere. Anything I can help you with?"

Bert Atkins had served Seminole County as sheriff until his second heart attack had forced him to retire, but his mind was as sharp as ever. With uncanny accuracy, he always knew when Tate was struggling with a problem.

Tate was, in fact, working on a suspected chop-shop operation, though that wasn't where his mind had been. He hadn't quite pinned down the source yet, but if he was right, the kingpin was a well-respected citizen. Bringing him down would be neither easy nor popular. And this was an election year.

After frowning at the board for a moment he moved his black king, jumping two of Bert's men. "Guess my mind isn't as scattered as you thought."

But to be honest, his mind *was* scattered. Julee Reynolds was driving him crazy. Since he'd found her slumped outside his door two days ago, looking like her dog had died, Tate had thought of little else. Having her name and the bone-marrow drive on the lips of every Blackwood citizen didn't help much and he was feeling like the county jerk instead of the county sheriff because he didn't want any part of either.

Bert slapped the table, sending the checkers into a quiver. "Gol' dern it, boy. I'm gonna have to study on this next move." He shoved a plastic bag in Tate's direction. "Here. Have a peppermint while I think."

Obliging, Tate removed the crinkling cellophane and welcomed the candy's cool sweetness. While Bert studied, his snow-white head bent over the board, Tate looked around at the group gathered in the Senior Room. A half dozen men played various games at other tables. He'd worked hard to gain the respect of this town, and in return the citizens of Blackwood had been good to him. He was happy, content. Or at least he had been until Julianna Reynolds blazed into town and reminded him of the hole inside his chest.

At the far end of the long room a group of ladies chatted

and crocheted around a sofa grouping. One of them looked up, caught his eye and waved. He knew by the way she elbowed her companion that the unattached sheriff of Seminole County had just become the topic of conversation.

With an inward groan, he waited. Who would it be this time? The new librarian? Or maybe Mary's recently divorced granddaughter? The ladies of Blackwood found his lack of a love life intensely interesting and seemed determined to remedy the problem by throwing unattached females in his path.

Sure enough, before Bert had a chance to claim any more of Tate's checkers, Mildred Perkins laid aside a long rectangle of pink fluff and headed in his direction. The busiest body in town, Mildred considered finding him a wife her sworn duty. They didn't understand what he couldn't tell them—he'd failed at love twice, and that was enough. He was good at a lot of things, but love wasn't one of them.

"Sheriff," Mildred began, fingering the eyeglasses that hung from a beaded chain around her neck.

"Mrs. Perkins," he acknowledged politely. "How are you and the Crochet Club today?"

"Oh, we've nearly finished that blanket for Cindy's new grandbaby. Which is what I wanted to see you about." She twisted the chain into a knot. "Not the baby exactly, but Cindy. Did you see the newspaper today? Cindy was right on the front page. Right there with Julianna Reynolds."

She said Julee's name with such relish Tate flinched.

He'd nearly swallowed a doughnut whole this morning when Rita had stuck the paper under his nose, berating him for not taking a more active part in Julee's charity blood drive. There was Julee, smiling fit to kill as she signed up folks for the big donor drive.

"Yes, ma'am. I saw that. Cindy looked mighty nice."

"Cindy?" Mildred's piercing voice shot up a notch. "Cindy? Land o' goshen, Sheriff, I'm not talking about Cindy. I'm talking about Julianna coming back to Blackwood to help cancer victims. Isn't that the sweetest thing you ever heard?"

"Yes, ma'am," he agreed, keeping a bland expression while hoping Mildred wasn't about to set him up with Julee. "Real nice of her."

"Did you know the car dealership is having a drawing? The winner gets to drive a new car free for a whole month?"

"I'd heard that." Who hadn't? In two days time, Julee had turned the entire town upside down. The radio station blasted a reminder of the bone-marrow drive every fifteen minutes, the newspaper couldn't seem to print enough rosy articles about the small-town girl who made good, and everywhere he went somebody reminded him of how sweet and perfect and *single* Julianna was. To hear them talk she was a cross between Mother Teresa and Sandra Bullock.

"Well?" Mildred crossed her arms over the huge red flower decorating her shirtfront and fixed him with a questioning stare.

He pinched his lips between thumb and forefinger and arched his eyebrows. Had he missed something?

"I didn't see your name on the list of civic leaders who've signed up to donate."

Tate sighed inwardly, guilt warming the back of his neck. He fiddled with a checker, sliding it back and forth along the edge of the board. "I didn't see yours, either."

"You gotta be under sixty," she huffed impatiently.

"And Lord knows I passed that a long time ago. You're young and fit as a fiddle so you got no excuse not to help out those poor little suffering children."

The guilt of worrying about those "poor little children" was eating a hole right through the smothered steak he'd had for lunch. "Needles make me nervous."

Mildred laughed and patted his arm. "Oh, Sheriff, you big tease. I know you'll do your part. Just have Julianna hold your hand while they poke you." She beamed at the genius of her suggestion. "And afterward, the two of you can come over to the Bingo Game together."

Bert clunked down another checker, taking one of Tate's. "Mildred, you're interfering with my concentration. Why don't you be useful and go get me a cup of coffee?"

While Tate silently thanked his old friend for the change of subject, Mildred drew back like a hissing adder. "Bert Atkins, you go get your own coffee."

With a huff, she flounced back to the circle of crocheting ladies who'd been acutely attentive during the brief exchange. Six smiles beamed their goodwill across the room. Mildred's mouth moved non-stop while she looked at Tate with an expression that said she was certain—absolutely certain—he wouldn't let her, or Julianna, down.

Sometimes Tate didn't know whether to hug them or hate them. Dear sweet ladies who meant well, but somehow thought he needed their input in every facet of his life. Not that he didn't appreciate their casseroles and pies and crocheted afghans. He did. But right now, the last thing he needed was another reminder of the woman he'd never been able to forget.

"Why not donate blood, Tate?" A checker in one hand, Bert paused. "Wouldn't be the first time."

Tate wallowed the peppermint with his tongue and pretended to study the checkers. "My deputies are helping out. I'm too busy to get wound up in Julee's celebrity tax write-off."

"Tax write-off or not, it's a good cause. Just because you and Julee were an item way back when is no reason to avoid her now. Unless you still have feelings for her."

Tate blanched at the plain speaking. Feelings? Heck, yes, he still had feelings for her. Trouble was, his feelings were all mixed up—fear, mistrust and a longing so fierce he'd been tormented all last night with dreams of Julee. He'd awakened in such a sweat he'd gotten up at 3:00 a.m. to take a shower. A cold one.

"As far as I'm concerned I'll be glad to see her gone."

"Question is, why?" Bert pointed a checker at him. "Shelly always said you never got over Julee."

How could he explain that avoiding Julee was a matter of self-preservation? Learning to live without her ten years ago had nearly killed him, an experience he couldn't afford to repeat.

"I wasn't the right man for Shelly," he said, skirting the issue of Julee. "You know it and so does she." His brief and disastrous marriage to Bert's daughter had been the final chapter in his book of love. Never again.

"A man can't work 24-7 and keep a woman happy, that's for sure."

"Running a sheriff's office is a full-time job. If anyone understands that, it's you."

"Being a good sheriff's one thing, but I don't recall ever sleeping in my office. You let this town run you ragged."

"I owe them, Bert. Just like I owe you."

The old sheriff had seen something worth saving in the rebellious youth, though for the life of him Tate couldn't imagine what it had been.

"You don't owe me a blamed thing. This county needed a good sheriff and we were danged lucky to get you."

"Still, I wish things could have been different for Shelly's sake."

"I know that, boy. That's why I got no hard feelings." Bert smiled and reached for another peppermint. "That and the fact that Shelly found a nine-to-five fellow and had me some grandbabies."

"She deserved a better man than me."

He'd married Shelly out of gratitude, like a groveling dog happy to have a pat on the head. She'd made him feel like a man again during those dark days when he'd cared more about killing himself with liquor and fighting than living, so he'd repaid her kindness by messing up her life. And the remorse he felt for disappointing his mentor, the only man who'd ever believed in him, would never go away.

He shook his head to clear the memory. As a rabble-rousing teenager he'd been called worthless trailer trash. Now he hid behind a clean uniform and a sheriff's badge, but deep down he figured the cruel taunt was still true.

Pushing back from the table, he looked at his wrist-watch. "Time to get back to work before the good citizens of Blackwood change their minds about me."

"Don't want to talk about Julee, huh?" Bert looked at him with a half smile.

"Nothing to talk about." He reached down to rub his knee. Thinking about Julee stirred up all his old aches and pains, some of them higher up than his knee. "She zoomed in here like a mosquito. Once she's zapped everyone's blood, she'll zoom right back out. The sooner, the better, as far as I'm concerned."

As he started to rise, the hospital administrator tapped in on low-heeled pumps to tack a huge poster on the bulletin board. Tate lifted a hand in greeting, then let it fall to the table, sinking back into his chair. A photo of Julee and her famous legs stared out at him below a caption announcing the bone-marrow drive. And if that wasn't enough to make him swallow the peppermint whole, the celebrity herself swept into the center, long, glorious legs drawing the stares of everyone in the place.

Julianna's heart took one giant leap from her chest to her throat. Tate, looking too handsome to be real, scowled at her from across a checkerboard. For the hundredth time since the meeting at his office, she asked herself why he disliked her so much. He'd been the one to betray her and find someone else in a painfully short amount of time. She'd known then that his love had not run as deep as he'd claimed.

Julee remembered the morning she'd left Blackwood like yesterday. Tate, wearing his high-school letter jacket, long black hair slicked into a ponytail, leaned his backside against a beat-up old Ford pickup, pulled her between the V of his legs and held her until the bus arrived.

She couldn't recall much of anything they'd said, just the feel of his rock-hard arms holding her close, the wool and leather scent of his jacket, and the warmth of his breath on her hair. The heavy ache of parting hung in the air between them. When the bus arrived, air brakes ripping the quiet morning, she'd started to cry. The Oklahoma wind had whipped her long hair around her face. Tate had smoothed it back, then cradled her face in his hands and brushed away the tears.

"Promise you'll come back," he whispered fiercely. "Promise."

Since the day she'd received the call from the Body Parts Agency in California, he'd agreed she had to go. He knew how badly she and her widowed mother needed the money this contract promised. No matter how much she loved Tate, this was a chance in a lifetime she had to take.

"I'll be back. I promise."

But the tormented look in his green eyes said he was just as scared as she was.

Heart breaking, she'd almost backed out, almost decided not to go when he pushed her up the steps.

"Go." He shoved twenty dollars in her hand and stepped back. "They're gonna love you out there."

As the double doors folded inward, he pressed two fingers to his lips and laid them on the window. She'd held his eyes, frantically mouthing "I love you, I love you," until the bus rumbled away and he was lost in the smoke and fumes. Hands shoved deep in his jacket pockets, he'd stared back at her with a stark, broken expression. She'd cried all the way to L.A., fearing that last kiss was his final farewell.

It had been. Regardless of his promise to wait, he'd found someone else and married before she'd even discovered she was pregnant with his child. So much for his promises of undying love. He'd moved on with his life and eventually so had she. So, why was he staring at her now as though she was a hair in his hamburger?

Self-conscious beneath his scrutiny, she smoothed both hands down the sides of her powder-blue sheath. Though she'd intentionally dressed to appear successful and confident, she felt as gawky and insecure as she had in high school, the skinny girl who was all legs.

To make matters worse, the hospital administrator, who was nearly as excited about the bone-marrow drive as she, drew the attention of everyone in the room. "Look, Julianna," she squealed. "There's the man you need."

Julee cringed. Oh, she needed him all right, though she

prayed he'd never find out just how much. Reluctantly, she left the woman's side and moved in Tate's direction. Since the disastrous meeting in his office, she'd steered clear, hoping public pressure would convince him to donate after she couldn't do the job. Now, time was growing short. She had to be certain he would be in town that day. If worse came to worst, she'd do the unthinkable. Against her mother's advice and at the risk of causing trouble for Tate and his wife, she'd tell him about Megan.

Approaching the table she recognized Bert Atkins, the man who'd been sheriff in her high-school days. Since arriving in Blackwood she'd renewed a number of old acquaintances, and though she didn't want to be here, had never planned to return, she was surprised to feel an unexpected nostalgia for her hometown.

"Hello, Mr. Atkins," she said cordially, training her eyes on him instead of Tate. Even then, she could imagine the heat of disapproval simmering from the county sheriff. Her pulse thudded disconcertingly.

"Howdy, Miss Julee. How's the big city?"

"Hectic. Noisy."

Bert grinned. "Yep, that's the way I remember cities."

"But L.A.'s a great city," she hurried to interject, not wanting him or Tate to know just how hectic life had become or how peaceful and pleasant Blackwood seemed after the crowded stress of L.A. "How about you? How's the family?"

"Good. Good. Shelly's a counselor over at the high school now and got two little ones, Zack and Amy. I'm a granddaddy."

A counselor. Julee's sense of worth dropped another notch. While she was flashing her legs for a camera, Tate's wife helped young people find direction and guidance.

And Tate had other children now. She glanced at him, but his green eyes were as hard and unreadable as marbles.

"I'm glad, Mr. Atkins. Tell her hello for me."

"You can tell her yourself. She'll be here the day of your big blood drive. I guess half the county will be."

"I hope so. That's what I needed to see the sheriff about."

"Well, sit down then." The older man hopped up and pulled out a chair. "You two go on and talk while I find me a cup of coffee." He glanced at Tate with a grin. "Guess Mildred isn't planning to bring me one."

Though she had no idea what he meant, Julee smiled in response and accepted the chair as Bert moved away, leaving her alone with Tate. For some reason, her legs grew weak every time she encountered Sheriff Congeniality. Scooting up to the table her knee bumped his, sending a warm awareness straight to her midsection. The contact had the opposite effect on Tate. He jerked as though she'd stabbed him.

Julee felt a trickle of remorse as realization struck. "Is it your knee?"

The question caught him by surprise. He blinked, reflexively reaching for the old injury. "No. The knee's fine."

"Oh. Good." An uncomfortable silence hung between them. After their initial encounter Julianna wasn't sure how to begin. What else could she possibly say to this familiar stranger that would change his mind?

"Could we declare a truce? Start all over?"

His right eyebrow shot up. "Start over?"

Closing her eyes momentarily she bit back a sigh. Once she'd been able to tell him anything, but now time and heartache had built a wall between them. "The hospital administrator tells me you're the man to see about traffic control.''

He shifted sideways, away from her. The fluorescent lights cast a glare along his square jawline, highlighting a narrow white scar. With a shock, she remembered the night he'd gotten that scar…because of her.

"Why would a blood drive require traffic control?''

Julee forced the memory away, though looking into his moss-green eyes proved just as tumultuous. "Because the high-school band has volunteered to drum up interest, if you'll pardon the pun, by marching down Main Street Saturday morning. People will hear the band and be reminded that the drive has begun.''

A gaggle of ladies, all carrying bags of yarn, twittered past, poking each other as they cast knowing looks at the handsome sheriff. Tate nodded politely, trying to cover an expression of amused exasperation.

"Look, Julee," he said, leaning near enough that she caught a whiff of peppermint and some wonderfully warm male scent. "I'm the sheriff, not a parade marshal. Can't the city police take care of that sort of thing?''

Julianna's pulse stumbled. From this close she could count the black spiky lashes framing Tate's green eyes. He had such beautiful eyes, deep and fathomless, and as full of mystery as the man himself.

Hands in her lap, she nervously twisted them together. Why was she thinking of Tate and that scar and his gorgeous eyes? Hadn't she had enough bad experiences with men? And why was she suddenly hub-deep in memories of the two of them jouncing along in that old beat-up Chevy truck, its heater barely keeping the fog off the windshield while they listened to Pearl Jam on their way to a football game? It was in that pickup that they'd first… Julianna mentally slammed on the brakes. *Do not go there.*

"The city police *are* helping," she said, amazed to sound so normal when her thoughts were anything but. "But they suggested your office was needed to erect detour barriers for through traffic and such things as that. In fact, Chief Little suggested the two of you coordinate efforts."

On an exhale Tate leaned back in his chair and glanced down at his watch. Light reflected off the handsome copper band with turquoise insets. "I'll talk to him."

Relieved, Julianna pressed clammy hands to the table-top. With any luck, she and the enthusiastic townspeople would wear down his resistance. Come Saturday, Tate would stretch out that dark, sinewy arm and give their daughter a new chance at life. "I appreciate this. I really do."

With an accepting tilt of his head, Tate's gaze fell to her hand. "That's quite a ring."

"Thank you." Nervously, she clasped the ringed hand to her chest, twisting the sapphire that matched her eyes.

"Engagement ring?"

"No."

He arched that black eyebrow again and she wished he'd stop it. The movement of that one little eyebrow had the power to reduce her to nothing. Embarrassed by her completely aberrant thoughts as well as the ostentatious sapphire, which had been a gift from a former beau, heat rushed to her cheeks. The cut and size of the stone weren't all that unusual in L.A. but here in Blackwood the ring seemed out of place. And so did she.

"So you're not married?" Behind the unfathomable eyes lurked an emotion Julee couldn't identify.

Uncomfortable with the personal turn of conversation, she gestured vaguely. "Not at the moment. My life is far too busy."

She didn't want to admit the truth, especially to Tate,

but the last man she'd dated had lost all interest when Megan's cancer returned. Though Julianna was too occupied with saving her daughter to mourn his loss, his disappearance had cemented her belief that she was only an ornament, a decoration.

"Too busy," he said softly, the words a reminder of how their own busy lives had pulled them in different directions.

The double doors leading into the center flapped open and a slight breeze swirled around their legs, bringing with it the scent of coffee and the remnants of the Chamber luncheon. A rattle of voices, the words incomprehensible, drifted around the room, but Julee felt isolated, captured in the aura of Tate McIntyre. An odd lump of longing filled her throat.

For a nanosecond the air vibrated with memory. Julee studied the remains of an interrupted checker game, making every attempt not to look at Tate.

Breaking the mood, Tate scraped back from the table and rose. "Sorry to run out on you again, but duty calls."

She looked up at him, grateful for the tiny crack in the fence between them. For one entire minute there had been a feeling, a *something* hovering around that table, that gave her hope. "Your job seems very important to you."

"It's my life." His wonderfully angled jaw clenched. "And I'm good at it, Julee. I'm *good* at it."

He turned to move away, his muscular legs long and fluid in the creased uniform pants.

"Tate," she called.

He turned back, waiting.

"I'm glad you've made a good life, that you're happy."

A flash of something—pain?—quickly masked, flared as he held her gaze. She didn't want to look at him, didn't want to feel the magnetism of Tate and the old memories, but she couldn't seem to tear her attention away. And truly she was pleased that the hurting boy she'd loved had found fulfillment.

"What about you?" he asked, his words intense, almost harsh. "Are you happy?"

"I…I…" Julee stuttered. "Of course."

"Good." For another interminable moment he held her with a look that brought a flush to her face and trepidation to her soul. And then he was gone, the beautiful athletic physique striding out of the Senior Center.

Why had he asked such a thing? And why had she hesitated? Her life was busy. She had her career, her friends. And most of all, she had Megan. Certainly, she was happy with the life she'd chosen.

Wasn't she?

Chapter Four

The day of the bone-marrow drive dawned with the perfect sunny weather of mid April in Oklahoma. Tate awoke, just as he did at least three times a week, in the front seat of his SUV. Only this morning the blast of the Blackwood High School marching band yanked him upright. He cracked his bad knee on the steering wheel and cursed. In the seat next to him a warm wiggling form yelped, reminding him of his only reward for a sleepless night.

Last night he'd sat inside a rusted-out station wagon inside the B & D Auto Salvage where he'd observed a transaction he could only view as suspicious. To his disappointment, no hard evidence of a chop-shop operation had come his way.

A warm wet tongue scraped at his hand.

"Hey, partner." With a grin, he stroked the skinny, red, mixed-breed pup he'd found scrounging around the Dumpsters outside B & D. He'd shared his chips and baloney with the mutt, but that had been hours ago. "I'll bet you're hungry as a bear.'' His own belly growled. ''I sure as heck am.''

Hoisting the pup like a football, he unlocked the side door to his office and, thankful for the facilities made available by his predecessor, went inside for a quick shower and shave. On his way he grabbed several pieces of ham from the small refrigerator in the employee's lounge.

''Here you go, fella.'' He laid the slices on a paper towel and filled a bowl with water. ''This'll have to do until we can get out to my place.''

Which wasn't likely to be soon. Tired as he was, today was the day of the bone-marrow drive. And he'd be glad when it was over. Then Julee and her famous legs could go back to L.A. and leave him the heck alone.

Not that she'd actually asked that much of him, but her presence in town had caused him no little discomfort. Everyone who remembered their romance brought it up. And everyone else seemed bound and determined to involve him in Julee's project. He didn't want to think about Julee and the rush of longing he experienced every time someone mentioned her name.

From outside, a tuba ripped off a few practice notes. He'd better hurry. He stepped into the closet-sized bathroom and shut the door.

Every man in town was agog over Julee. Big deal. What man wouldn't be enthralled by her combination of beauty, smarts and success? Just because she wasn't married now didn't mean she hadn't been a half dozen times before. And even if she'd had as many lovers as his mother, her private life was none of his business. But he'd gone off spouting about happiness like a love-starved orphan. He'd had to bite the inside of his lip to keep from asking if she was dating anyone. And if she was, was he good to her?

Did he make her laugh? Would he give her the houseful of kids she'd always wanted?

Stripping off his clothes he kicked the wrinkled jeans into the corner in disgust.

There he went again assuming she was still the same Julee he'd known, when she clearly wasn't. Back then she'd dreamed of two things—making enough money to take care of her mother and then spending the rest of her life with him and the babies they would make together. Now, family was the last thing on her mind.

He'd known then the dream was too good to be true and that he'd lose her to California, proving what he'd always known. A shanty-town bastard with a chip on his shoulder wasn't good enough for her or any decent woman. That was okay. He'd accepted who he was and all his shortcomings a long time ago. He didn't deserve her, never had.

She'd been so good, his Julee. The kind of girl who championed the underdog, stood up against bullies. He smiled at that, remembering how she'd stood up to him a few times when he'd wanted to break some guy's nose just because he was mad at the world. Sensible, gentle Julee had a calming effect on the wild, angry boy he'd been. She could make him do anything.

But not this time. Not again. He nearly hadn't survived the last time. He couldn't fall under her spell again.

He grabbed a towel from the tiny corner cupboard and turned the shower on full blast.

He had to get Julee out of his mind and out of his town. If he could keep his distance another twenty-four hours she'd be gone. Stepping beneath the spray, he let the warm water drown every thought of Julianna Reynolds.

In minutes, smelling and feeling considerably better and dressed in the extra uniform he kept hanging on the back of the bathroom door, Tate was out on the street. The stray pup attached his nose to the sheriff's creased pant leg and followed.

This morning the usually early sheriff was late, a fact that disgruntled him no end. To make matters worse, Julee stood in the middle of Main Street talking to his deputies. So much for washing her out of his mind. Every cell in his body started to hum. Criminy. Why'd she have to look like that?

"Mornin', boss." Jeet waved a doughnut in his direction. Tate's stomach growled again. He'd given the last of the ham to the pup. "What's that thing following you? A piece of rusted baling wire?"

Glad for the distraction, Tate's mouth quirked at the apt description of the skinny pup dogging his heels. "Ah, just a stray I picked up last night."

"Another one?" Jeet's fleshy jowls jiggled as he turned toward Julee. She looked beyond beautiful standing in the morning sun with her long brown hair gently blowing around her face. "The sheriff here's got a dozen of these mutts running around his place. Supposed to turn them over to animal control, but he never does."

The pup, as though terrified by the thought, rushed to the nearest fire hydrant and lifted his leg. When Tate slanted a glance toward Julee and found her holding back a laugh, he relented and grinned.

"Stupid mutt."

She giggled, a fresh sound that made his stomach lift. Just what he needed. More reminders of the teenage Julee. For some reason, he thought she would have lost that hiccoughing giggle in the slick professional atmosphere of California.

"Do you really have a dozen strays at your place?" A wisp of hair blew across her mouth, clinging momentarily to the soft, rosy smudge of color. Mesmerized, he watched her push it back, remembering the softness, the heat of those lips.

The *bom, bom, bom* of a bass drum brought him to his senses. Pulling his gaze from her face, Tate hardened his resolve not to be affected by her kissable lips or her million-dollar legs.

"Not quite a dozen," he said grudgingly.

"How many?" Unmindful of his inner turmoil she pressed, blue eyes twinkling up at him in the morning sun.

"Too many."

"Why not let animal control take them?"

He frowned and her smile disappeared. Lots of dogs around town were euthanized but not the ones on his shift. Though he didn't expect Julianna Reynolds to understand that. "Even a stray deserves a chance."

Her kissable lips formed an *O*.

"You mean, animal control would—?" With a grimace, she stroked a finger across her throat.

"Yeah."

"That's awful."

Julee crouched down to pet the dog as it sidled up to her, pink tongue lolling. As her long nails stroked the animal, Tate felt an unwelcome response in his gut. This morning Julee was dressed in a straight red skirt he considered too short, though he figured every man in town would argue the point. Her legs were her claim to fame and from the looks of her, she didn't mind using them to get what she wanted. Once she'd have been embarrassed at such attention, but as he kept reminding himself, this was a different Julee altogether. Polished, self-assured, she was every inch the successful California model, and he was still the country boy from the wrong side of town.

Tearing his thoughts from Julee and her legs, he glanced

up and down the street, noting with relief that the barriers were in place, the ropes strung across intersections to keep traffic out during the brief parade. "Looks like everything is ready."

"Yep. Miss Reynolds wouldn't let us rest until it was." Jeet beamed a besotted smile at Julee. "She was here before daylight."

Daylight? He had to hand it to Julee; she wasn't afraid of hard work and long hours. All week, to his dismay, every time he'd looked up she'd come whipping around the corner to recruit someone else to her cause. Though he'd successfully run a political campaign, he'd never observed such effective and efficient organizational skills.

From her crouched position beside the pup, Julee returned Jeet's smile. With great discipline Tate refrained from staring at her legs.

"You've all done a fabulous job. A lot of good will come from your efforts." She gave the little dog one last stroke and rose. "I don't know how to thank you."

Jeet's beam grew wider. "Heck fire, Miss Reynolds, we're just tickled to have you back in town. This drive of yours has got the whole county buzzing."

Tate grimaced at the adulation.

"Say, Miss Reynolds," Jeet went on. "Would you like an escort over to the Community Center? I'd be honored to take you in my car after the street clears."

"You'd better stick around here with me, Jeet," Tate found himself saying. "Just in case your wife shows up."

Jeet blushed crimson and Tate wished he'd kept his cranky mouth shut. But good grief! The deputy was making a fool of himself over a woman who would forget his name before her plane touched down at LAX.

A siren split the air and a city police car made its way

down the street as a signal to clear the path. The pup yelped, tucked his tail and shimmied up Tate's pant leg.

"Here they come," Julee exclaimed. Clapping her hands over her ears, she hopped onto the sidewalk beside Tate.

Hoisting the quivering dog beneath one arm, Tate watched Julee and her parade. Her elegant perfume scented the fresh spring morning and her eyes glowed with a fanatical passion that made him wonder. She'd always been passionate. A passionate champion of the underdog. Passionate in her desire to make a better life for her mother and herself. Passionate in his arms. But this was different.

"Looks like you'll get a good turnout," he said above the noise.

Julee glanced up, her blue eyes nearly level with his. The fire of hope burned bright in their depths. "Does that mean you'll take part? Say you will, Tate. Please." She clutched his arm with an expression that shook him. "You could be the person to save someone's precious child."

Tate pried the red mutt out from under his armpit and squirmed uncomfortably. It was happening to him. One more minute, one more of her eager blue-eyed looks and he'd fall under her spell again. Only the discipline he'd learned the hard way enabled him to utter his oft-repeated excuse. "I don't get along too well with needles."

Some of her glow dimmed. Gnawing at her bottom lip, she loosened her hold and turned back toward the street, dejected.

Tightness banded Tate's chest. Once they'd stood on this very street corner and watched the homecoming parade, his arm slung over her shoulders, hers around his waist. That night he'd fumbled the touchdown pass that would have won the game, but afterward Julee had been there for him, comforting him.

Now he wanted so badly to comfort her, to explain. Yet, the truth was he couldn't explain what he didn't fully understand. The only thing he was sure of was how dangerous it was for him to be anywhere near her.

"Julee," he began softly. *Fool, fool, fool,* his brain chanted.

Blue eyes filled with hope and pain and fear met his, and again he wondered what demons chased Julianna Reynolds.

"Yes?"

Before he had a chance to say something he was certain to regret, fate intervened. The high-school marching band, resplendent in red-and-white uniforms, paraded by, blasting out an energetic version of "Another One Bites the Dust." Over the drums and the tubas and the trombones, he heard a shout.

"Sheriff!"

Tate whirled toward the sound.

A couple of hardheaded teenagers, not unlike the boy he'd once been, had chosen this morning to vent their frustrations outside the Hamburger Hangout. A teenage girl stood nearby, crying and shouting while the boys flailed at one another.

Grateful for the opportunity to escape, Tate loped toward the fight.

Sometime later, when he finally arrived at the Community Center, Tate could hardly believe his eyes. In a carnival-like atmosphere, the citizens of Seminole County swarmed around the transformed parking lot like happy honeybees. A raucous beat throbbed from a flatbed trailer as the high-school cheerleaders performed an energetic dance routine. Nearby, the scent of barbecue wafted from the Boy Scouts' smoker. Tate's belly reacted with a growl.

The mutt must have felt the same for he looked longingly in that direction and whined, his thin tail working overtime.

"Soon, fella," Tate murmured. Even the dog had to understand that duty came before anything else. Once he'd made the rounds and checked in with the other law-enforcement groups he'd feed himself and the pup.

He headed toward the far end of the parking lot where uniformed medical personnel escorted children through an ambulance and a life-flight helicopter. From there, the kids climbed into the fire department's "smoke house," a unit designed to teach them to exit a burning building safely.

He was impressed. Julee's blood drive was doing far more good for the community than he'd imagined.

Stopping frequently to greet the townspeople, while keeping an eye on his peacekeeping duties, Tate made his way around the area. But no matter where he went or who he talked with, his attention always came back to one spot.

Right smack in the middle of all the activity was a bloodmobile. The glamorous Miss Reynolds stood outside in her too-short skirt, smiling a million-dollar smile. All day long she moved up and down the endless line of prospective blood donors shaking hands, handing out I Donated stickers, and occasionally tossing back her long brown hair to laugh.

With grudging admiration he realized she'd done it. In a week's time she'd pulled together enough civic groups to draw a huge crowd of people to her cause. The smallest group was the Seminoles, the people Julee specifically wanted to register. There was a mild turnout, thanks to the few phone calls he'd made, but with a twinge of guilt Tate knew he could have done more. He had great rapport with the tribal bands, and though they jokingly called him an "apple"—red on the outside, white on the inside—his total involvement would have guaranteed more people.

Full of remorse, he saw just how wrong he'd been to let his confused feelings for Julee cloud his sense of right. He should have done more. Little kids with cancer shouldn't suffer because he was lousy at love.

He glanced around for the mutt. The drive lasted until seven. With four hours left he had time to make more calls.

"Sheriff McIntyre." Timothy, a third grader from his Little League team, tugged on his arm.

Tate hunkered down beside the boy. "Hey, Tim. What's up?"

"Jeremy says it hurts bad to give blood. Is that true?"

Tate studied the solemn freckled face. Jeremy was Tim's eighteen-year-old brother. "Did Jeremy donate?"

"Yeah," Timothy breathed in amazed admiration. "And he's got a Band-Aid on his arm."

"That was mighty brave of Jeremy to want to help other people that way."

"Yeah." Timothy dropped his head. "He said only a *man* could give blood and I was just a little pip-squeak who couldn't do nothing for nobody. I wish I could, though. I would if I could."

"I know you would, bud."

"You're going to, ain't ya, Sheriff?" the boy asked eagerly. "You'll let 'em take blood out of both your arms, I'll bet. That'll show Jeremy he ain't the bravest man in town."

Tate's heart squeezed at the open hero worship. When he was a kid, he'd have given anything for a father figure to admire and respect. Instead, he'd had to fight everyone who had called his mother a whore, while longing for the day his father would appear and lay claim to him. It had never happened. Though his mother admitted what his face told him—that he was part Seminole—she'd never given him a father to adore.

Clasping Timothy on the shoulder, Tate's gaze drifted back to Julee, now talking earnestly with the mayor. She seemed to sense his attention because she looked up and caught him staring. She smiled and his heart lifted foolishly.

"Huh, Sheriff? Are you going to?"

If he did, would the guilt of not helping more go away? Would he stop wanting to pull Julee into his arms and shield her from the anxiety he felt in her?

With a self-deprecating shake of his head Tate gazed at the adoring boy. "If I do, will you watch my dog?"

Julee could barely tear her eyes away from the tall, popular sheriff who stared at her over the top of a small boy's head. Something in her reacted wildly to the picture of him with a fatherly hand on the child's shoulder. Would he have been a good daddy to their daughter?

He was a good politician; that was for certain. And something she'd never have believed if she hadn't watched him all afternoon. Watching him had nothing at all to do with the fact that he was gloriously handsome and wonderfully warm and friendly to everyone. No matter that he'd hurt her so badly all those years ago, he was Megan's father, and she needed to know what kind of man he'd become. That was the only reason she couldn't take her eyes off him.

"That sheriff sure is something, isn't he?" The hospital administrator had come out of the bloodmobile to stand beside Julee. "Little kids are crazy about him."

"He must be a wonderful father."

"Would be if he had any kids."

Julianna frowned. "But I thought— Don't he and Shelly have two children?"

"Good land, Julee, this is old news, but I guess you don't know it." The woman stared at her, incredulous. "Shelly and Tate only stayed together a couple of years. Shelly married Larry Wilkins about five years ago and has two kids with him."

"I have been gone a long time, haven't I?" She tried to laugh it off, to sound disinterested, but her insides went crazy at the implication. Tate wasn't married, hadn't been for a long time.

The hospital administrator moved on, washed away in the crowd, but Julianna's focus remained on Tate. He wasn't married? Hadn't been for years? She watched him more intently now, blood humming in her temples.

A swarm of little boys had followed him around the parking lot off and on all day, hero worship on their faces. At noon he'd bought them sandwiches and soft drinks, even feeding the bedraggled little pup a hotdog. More than one attractive woman had stopped him, too, and he'd talked and laughed with them, his smile white against mocha skin.

Feeling a sense of loss at the wide gap between herself and the father of her child, she ran a weary hand through her hair and turned back toward the bloodmobile. Tate couldn't stand the sight of her, couldn't wait for her to leave town. One thing for sure, no matter how much she dreaded the confrontation, now that she knew he had no family, if he didn't give blood before this day was over she would tell him that he had a daughter.

Moving up the steps, she went inside the cool, quiet unit to take her turn at passing out juice. To her satisfaction, all the booths were filled with donors. With every tube of blood drawn Julianna rejoiced for some mother somewhere who wouldn't have to go through this agony of fruitless searching.

Relieving the orange juice volunteer, she readied a half dozen paper cups for the line of people coming through the doors. As she handed a cup to one of the firefighters, the door opened and a tall uniformed figure ducked in from the sunshine.

When the county sheriff removed a gray Stetson Julee's heart skittered to a stop, then started again, pounding wildly. Her hand shook, slopping juice onto the friendly firefighter.

"Oh! I'm sorry." Grabbing a paper towel, she blotted the mess on the man's pant leg. All the while her attention remained riveted to the front of the bloodmobile.

The firefighter chuckled and grabbed her hand. With her preoccupation with Tate, she'd strayed too far up the thigh. "I gotta say, ma'am, getting juice spilled on me has never been so much fun, but we do have an audience."

Embarrassed and jubilant at the same time, she gave the firefighter another towel, apologized again, and moved to the next donor.

Tate was inside the bloodmobile. She struggled to hold back the exultant tears. He was here. Did that mean…?

"I hate needles," Tate declared to the pretty blond technician in turquoise scrubs.

"You're in good hands, Sheriff. I'm the best."

He cocked his finger and pointed it at the woman. "You'd better be or you're under arrest."

The technician laughed. "What's the charge?"

"Assaulting an officer of the law."

With a stab of envy Julee observed the teasing exchange. Years ago, she'd seen flashes of this side of him, though he was much more mellow and gentle now than he had been then.

Obviously flirting with the handsome sheriff, the technician laughed again and led him to the first available booth. With some difficulty, Tate managed to fold his long legs into the narrow space. A grimace of pain came and went as he settled in, and Julee thought his knee must bother him a lot more than he let on.

He stretched his long, muscular arm along the small counter provided for that purpose. A wild thrill of joy shot through Julee.

He was going to do it. He was going to save Megan's life.

Heart jackhammering, Julee watched the procedure with the interest of a starving vampire.

Absently handing out more juice as she went, Julianna edged toward the booth where Megan's life hung in the balance. With every drop of Tate's rich dark blood that flowed into the tube, hope lifted, her mother's heart certain he was the match Megan needed. Everything would be all right now. Tate had finally agreed to give his blood, and she was convinced he'd give his bone marrow when the time came. And patient confidentiality would keep him from ever knowing that he'd saved his own daughter's life.

Nothing could go wrong now. Absolutely nothing.

Chapter Five

Julee paced the plush peach carpet of her Los Angeles condominium waiting for the telephone call that would save her daughter's life. Today was the day they'd know if Tate matched. Though she'd called the lab no less than four times already and had been promised a return call as soon as the test results were completed, she didn't think she could bear the suspense much longer. Ready to fly into a million pieces, she had barely eaten or slept since the return from Oklahoma.

The bone-marrow drive had proven successful beyond her wildest dreams, though she was still stunned to discover Tate had been divorced for nearly eight years. Getting his donation would have proven much easier if she'd known, but the end result was the same. She'd not only gotten Tate to donate, but she'd succeeded in adding a large number of Native Americans to the national database. The knowledge that other children would benefit filled her with joy. For a while she'd feared the Seminoles wouldn't come, but during the remaining few hours a steady stream of beautiful dark faces had filed into the unit to share their life's blood with some needy person somewhere.

Now the day of truth had arrived and her head throbbed from the waiting. She was glad to know the bone-marrow drive would help sick children all over the country, but today she'd know if one of those children was her own.

Crossing to the glass curio cabinet, she lifted Megan's latest photo from the shelf. Luminous green eyes glowed above a smile almost wider than the narrow face. She hugged the picture frame to her chest, thankful Megan remained well enough to attend school. Julee wasn't certain she could have hidden her anxiety from the little girl who'd learned to be wise beyond her years.

"Honey, wearing a hole in the carpet won't make the phone ring any sooner."

Beverly Reynolds finished folding a towel, laid it on the growing stack on the pastel-flowered divan, and looked up at her daughter with empathetic eyes.

"I don't understand why they haven't called." Carefully, she replaced the photo.

"They'll call. As soon as—"

The jangling telephone stopped the flow of words.

"Oh, Lord." Julee clutched at her chest. "Oh, Lord."

The phone jangled again.

Frozen, she shot a wild look at her mother. "I'm afraid to answer it."

Beverly rose, as tense as Julee. "Shall I?"

"No." Knees quaking, Julee stumbled to the glass-and-wicker end table and yanked the receiver off the hook.

"Hello." Her pulse shot up. It was the lab. Hands trembling, she shoved the hair away from her face.

Her ears began to buzz. Black spots danced around the cool white-and-peach living room. Julianna gripped the wall to keep from falling.

"Yes. I understand. Yes. I know. Thank you for calling."

Slowly, grappling to maintain her hold on sanity, she placed the telephone into the cradle and turned to her mother. Beverly waited with an expression of mingled hope and fear.

Staggering, barely able to breathe, Julee reached out. Trembling violently, her legs gave way and she went to her knees on the carpet as the hideous words spewed forth.

"He's not a match. He's not a match." The cry became a groan. "Oh, God, Mama, Tate doesn't match."

"No! Oh, sweetheart." Tears welled in her mother's eyes as she dropped to the floor and pulled Julee into her embrace. Shaking and crying, both women gave vent to despair.

"My baby. My baby," Julee wailed. "Oh, Mama, my baby is going to die. She's going to die. And I can't stop it."

As her last hope for a cure disappeared, the solid comfort of her mother's arms kept her from shattering like crystal on concrete. She'd been so certain that Tate would match, that he would donate his bone marrow and give their beautiful child a second chance at life. How could this happen? And what could she do now?

Devastated beyond words, the mother and daughter rocked together, back and forth, back and forth, like two rudderless ships in a hurricane. The telephone rang twice and the buzzer sounded on the clothes dryer, but still they rocked, crying and wailing until the sobs faded to throbbing whimpers.

For the rest of her life Julianna would remember the scent of fabric softener emanating from the stacks of Megan's clean clothes. Just as she'd recall the hot torrent of her mother's tears dampening the front of her silk shell.

She couldn't bear it. She simply couldn't go on.

Chest convulsing with sorrow, Julianna lifted her head. All around her lay the trappings of years of hard work. Elegant furnishings, beautiful clothes, and beyond the open drapes of the patio door, a swimming pool glistening turquoise in the California sun. Propped at the end of one chaise lounge was Megan's lime-green air mattress.

Defeated, she closed her eyes.

All the money in all the banks in California could not save the most important person in the world—her little girl.

Hot tears started up again. The carpet fibers pressed into her knees but she was beyond caring. What did her perfect legs matter without Megan?

In desperate need of a tissue Julee pulled away, blotting her face with both palms. Her throat hurt and her swollen eyes burned. On her mother's face she saw the same sense of hopeless despair, and her heart broke all over again.

"Why is this happening?" She dropped her head back and moaned. "Was it this place? Did living here in this smog-infested city make my daughter sick?"

"No, darling. No."

"What caused it then? Me? Did I do something wrong before she was born?" She stared around wildly, remembering. "I didn't eat right, and I was nervous and scared all the time, trying so hard to succeed in modeling. Did I damage her cells? Is that what happened? Did I do this to my child and now God is punishing her for my mistakes?"

The questions had haunted her for a long time, though she'd never given voice to her worries until now. As a teenager, she'd never been regular, and with the stress of the modeling contract and her naturally long, thin body she'd been over five months pregnant before she realized she was carrying Tate's child.

"Shh. Stop that. That's nonsense and I won't listen to it." Her mother gave her shoulders a little shake. "Listen to me, Julianna. We will not give up. We can't give up. Somebody out there has to be a match. We'll keep going, keep searching. There has to be a way to save our girl."

Hardly able to breathe, Julee clawed at her chest, the edge of panic fast closing in. "I wish I'd had more children. I wish I'd married long ago and had a house full. If I hadn't come to L.A., if Tate and I had married, if we'd had more children. Surely one of them would have been a match."

"Hush, Julee." Her mother reached to embrace her. "Hush, now. You're getting hysterical."

Disconsolate, Julianna backed away from Beverly's comfort. How could she be comforted when her life was unraveling right before her eyes? "If I hadn't been so selfish. If I hadn't moved out here to pursue a career."

"Julianna Rene, you listen to me and you listen good. After your Daddy died, I held things together as long as I could, but you and I both know that modeling contract was an answer to a prayer. You didn't accept that contract for yourself. You did it for us. We needed that money to survive."

Though she recognized the truth in her mother's words, Julianna couldn't shake the feeling that her bad choices were now costing Megan her life. "But what is money without family? I foolishly thought I could have it all. Money, marriage, kids. If I had married Tate, Megan would have had the brothers and sisters she always wanted."

"You were both too young, and Tate was too angry and wounded. A marriage between you two would have been disastrous."

"But you should see him now, Mama. Somehow he

vercame all the pain of his childhood to become a decent
nd good man. He would have been a wonderful father.''

"We can't change the past, honey."

Julianna crossed to the patio doors and pressed her fore-
ead into the cool glass. Mama was right. She couldn't
hange the past. She couldn't go back ten years and have
nore children with the boy she'd loved so passionately.

Suddenly, the shadow of an idea, an idea too preposter-
us to consider, shifted and began to take form.

"Mama," she started, slowly turning away from the
lant-bedecked patio. "You remember last night while
Megan was reading her story to me?"

Her mother nodded, a frown of puzzlement forming
bove her red-rimmed eyes.

"Lying on that bed, I looked at my little girl, felt her
ony ankles twined around mine, and the love inside me
early exploded my chest. I would do anything—anything,
Mama, to save her life."

"I know you would. And so would I." Beverly's shoul-
ers slumped. "If we only knew what that something
vas."

Excitement mingled with stark fear spurted adrenaline
nto Julianna's blood. Had she finally lost what little mind
he had left? Was she mad to be thinking like this?

"What if there is something we can do? What if I can
lmost certainly provide a donor for Megan?"

Gnawing the side of her lower lip, Beverly pushed her
air behind one ear. "Is such a thing possible?"

"I think so." Julianna's heart thumped painfully against
er rib cage. Would her mother be horrified? "Promise
ou won't hate me for what I'm about to suggest."

"I could never hate you, but honey, you're making me
ervous. You don't have anything illegal in mind, do
ou?"

Illegal? No. But was it wrong? Was she evil and immoral for having such a thought? Or was she only a desperate mother willing to do anything to save her child?

"What if Megan had a brother or sister? What if Tate and I had another child together?"

Beverly blinked in bewilderment. "But that's not possible. You don't even know Tate anymore. You've..." Beverly stopped, studying her daughter through clear blue eyes. Her mouth dropped open in stunned realization.

"Are you saying what I think you're saying?" she asked incredulously.

"I've been hearing about cord blood transplants, Mom. I'd have to ask Dr. Padinsky for details, but from what I understand a transplant of cord blood from a sibling is always a match. Couples have done it before—had a second baby to save the first. If I had another child with Tate..."

"Julee." Her mother held up a palm, astonished. "What are you saying? You and Tate aren't a couple."

Collapsing onto the cushiony sofa, Julianna covered her face with both hands. "I know, I know," she moaned. "You must think I'm losing my mind. But I don't know what else to do."

Beverly came to sit beside her, draping an arm around Julianna's trembling shoulders. "No, honey, I don't think you're losing your mind. You're just frantic and distraught and desperate to save that incredible granddaughter of mine."

"Megan has run out of options and we both know this remission can't last much longer." Tears clogged the back of Julee's throat. "I can't lose her. If I let her die without doing everything in my power to save her, I'll never forgive myself. She's worth everything. Everything."

The tears spilled over and soft sobs shook her again.

Beverly leaned back against the fluffy couch. A heavy pall hovered over the room. After an extended silence, she released a long, slow breath.

"Yes," she said with quiet determination. "You're absolutely right. Megan is worth whatever we have to do to save her. And if that means asking that McIntyre boy to give you another child, then so be it."

Startled by the change of heart, Julianna searched her mother's expression and found only loving acceptance in the sky-blue eyes. A seed of hope sprang up. "Are you certain?"

Kneading the back of her neck, Beverly looked toward the ceiling. In a low voice, she said, "We have no other choice."

Tormented with the enormity of such a decision, Julianna pressed her hot cheeks. "But is it wrong? If Tate agreed to father another child with me, would it be a sin?"

Even if her mother said yes, God forgive her, Julianna would still do it. She would trade her own soul for Megan's life if that's what it took.

"How can saving the life of another human being be wrong?" Beverly asked.

"But what about the baby? Is it wicked to create a child for the express purpose of saving another?"

She could hardly believe they were having this conversation. The idea was preposterous, unthinkable, and yet, here she sat, warring within while actually considering the possibility.

"Unfortunately, children have been conceived with much less forethought than this."

"But a child deserves to be special, to be wanted and loved just because he exists."

"Oh, my darling girl. Don't you know yourself better than that? Any child you carry beneath your heart for nine months will be loved as fiercely and wondrously as you love Megan.'' Beverly took Julianna's hand and stroked the long trembling fingers. ''Know that, honey. *Know that.*''

Was her mother right? She had always wanted more children. With an agonized sigh, she absorbed her mother's words, grappling with the hope that her radical idea was, perhaps, not as unconscionable as she'd feared.

''Most of us live our entire lives wondering why we're here, what our purpose is. Megan's brother or sister would always know that his or her purpose was the most special of all. The baby would bring the gift of life for his or her sister. What could be more wonderful than knowing that?''

Closing her eyes, Julianna prayed with all her heart that what Mama said was true. Because, right or wrong, Julee knew what she must do. In order to give Megan a future, she had to return to Blackwood and ask Tate McIntyre to make another baby.

The cacophony of barking dogs brought Tate out of the kitchen and to the front door. From his experience, early morning news was never good.

A late-model Toyota, a rental from the looks of it, sat in his front drive. The headlights winked off, and even in the pink-gray dawn he recognized the occupant. His stomach did a nosedive. Julee.

Cursing the unwanted quickening in his blood, he stepped out onto the long porch that ran the length of his modest ranch-style house.

''Dogs,'' he commanded. ''Hush!''

The half dozen or so mutts stopped barking and raced toward him, groveling and smiling, to press wiggling bodies against his legs. With a forgiving grin, he reached down and scratched the closest head, keeping both eyes trained on the white Toyota.

Julee opened her car door and slid long, elegant legs onto the ground, then came across the dewy green grass. Dressed in dark slacks and a sky-blue pullover sweater, her long hair loose and flowing, she looked all of sixteen in the pale dawn.

"What's wrong?" he called before she made it to the porch.

She looked up, surprised. "How do you know something's wrong?"

"Why else would you be here—" He glanced at his turquoise and copper watch, the only article of clothing on his upper body "—at six o'clock in the morning?"

"I need to talk to you. It's urgent."

"Figured as much." He waved her inside. "I was fixing coffee. Would you like a cup?"

"Yes. Thank you."

Once she stepped into the lighted room, he noticed the signs of strain around her eyes and mouth, and the worry in her eyes. Something was definitely wrong. But what did it have to do with him?

To his surprise she followed him into the kitchen, her subtle perfume blending with the scent of fresh-brewed coffee. Though the country-sized kitchen was clean, he figured his home looked pretty bare and poor compared to her fancy place in California. Not that he cared. He loved this place, had worked his tail off to buy it, and he wouldn't trade one acre of his land for all the beachfront property in Malibu. Still, seeing his home through Julee's eyes bothered him. It was a reminder that she'd been right to leave, that he could never have given her all the nice things she wanted.

"Sugar?" He held up the sugar bowl.

"Please."

"You look like you could use a couple of doughnuts, too." If such a thing was possible, she was thinner than she had been a couple of weeks ago. "And a shot of bourbon, instead of coffee."

The silly combination made her smile. "Coffee will do."

He handed her the cup, then led the way to the small chunky wooden table by the window. "Have a seat while I find a shirt."

When he returned to the kitchen, dragging a white T-shirt over his head, Julianna was sitting hunched over her coffee cup, looking like a lost kid. Scraping back his chair, he slid into the seat and wrapped both hands around his warm coffee mug.

"So. Are you going to tell me?" He studied the tense set of her shoulders. "Or do I have to interrogate you like a criminal?"

When she favored him with another tired smile, his stomach went south. She looked exhausted.

"Thanks," she said.

"For what?"

"For being nice. For making this easier."

"You caught me on a good day." For the first time in weeks he actually had a day off. And last night a major donor had signed up to support his campaign for re-election. Except for finding Julianna Reynolds on his doorstep at sunrise, life was going well. "So. Are you going to tell me what brings you back to Blackwood for the second time in less than a month?"

"Yes. But I don't know how." The white tips of her fingernails trembled against the cup handle. "For days I've tried to think of the best way, of the words that would make it easier, and I still don't know." Blue eyes wide with anxiety searched his.

Her full rose-tinted lips quivered, and Tate fought a sinking sensation. Something serious was going on here. And he had a real bad feeling about it.

"Does it have anything to do with the bone-marrow drive?"

"Yes." She shook her head. "No."

When he quirked an eyebrow, she clarified, "The drive wasn't a celebrity tax write-off, Tate. It was personal."

"Ah." Now they were getting somewhere. He leaned back in his chair and studied her, his chest tight. Was she sick? "How personal?"

She swallowed, throat working against the elegant column of her neck. "My daughter has leukemia. Without a bone-marrow transplant she'll die."

The ugly words thundered in the quiet kitchen. Outside one of the dogs thumped against the front door and another yelped. With a wince of compassion, Tate set his coffee cup on the table. "I'm sorry. I didn't know you had a daughter."

No wonder she'd been so fanatical about the drive. He had never heard about her marriage much less that she had a child, and while he wanted to resent the revelation, he was too concerned about the tragedy of her sick daughter. Julee'd always wanted kids and he knew she'd fight like a tiger to take care of a sick one.

She looked up, blue eyes glistening with unshed tears. "Her name is Megan, and she's beautiful. Oh, Tate, she's so precious. I can't let her die."

"I'm sorry, Julee. I really am." He leaned forward, stretching a hand across the table, wanting to touch her but afraid of letting her know just how much she affected him. "My heart goes out to you and I'd like to help, but

I'm having a hard time understanding why you'd come to me about your daughter.''

"Not just *my* daughter, Tate." Julee lay her icy fingertips atop his hand. "*Our* daughter."

"*Our* daughter?" He blinked, uncomprehending. "What are you talking about?"

"When I left here nearly ten years ago, I was carrying your baby."

"A daughter?" He felt like he'd been sucker punched. "My God in Heaven! I have a little girl?" With the wind knocked out of him, he dropped back into the chair and sat there, arms lax, too shocked to speak.

The alarm on his watch sounded. Absently, he clicked it off. Who cared what time it was?

Taking a deep breath, he thrust a hand over the tips of his hair, sliding the fingers to the back of his head where he held on, trying to keep from losing his mind.

He had a little girl.

"She has your eyes."

Tate's body jerked. His hand fell to his lap. A dozen questions crowded his mind. Why? Why hadn't she told him? And why was she telling him now?

He wanted to be furious, to rage at Julee for her deceit, but he was too stunned and too scared. He had a daughter in California. With his eyes. And his blood. He looked down at his arms and realization struck.

"Am I a match? Is that why you're here?" He pushed back from the table and jumped up. "I'll do it. Let's go, right now. She can have anything of mine. Anything that will help her. Give me five minutes and I'll be packed."

He started around the table. Julee grabbed his arm as he passed her chair.

"Tate. No." Her white-tipped nails grazed his skin.

Tears swam in her haunted blue eyes. "You're not a match. No one is."

He'd been in a bar brawl once when a biker the size of a house had stomped his rib cage. He felt like that now.

He had a daughter he'd never seen. She was dying and he couldn't do a thing to help her. He went down on his knees beside Julee. The bad knee protested, but he refused to give in to the pain. A little girl with his eyes knew a lot more about pain than he'd ever understand.

"I'll find her a donor, Julee." He gripped her hands. They were ice-cold. "We'll have more blood drives, all over the state. All over the country if that's what it takes. But we'll find her a match."

Julee shook her head. A single tear seeped over dark lashes and Tate fought the need to brush it away, to make her all kinds of foolish promises. "We've been looking for months. Finding a non-related donor at this point would take a miracle. And we don't know how much more time we have."

Defeated, he tipped backward onto his heels and stared up at the ceiling. A glorious sunrise broke through the double windows behind the table, but despair—dark and heavy—blotted the dazzling light.

Tate's mind reeled with confused emotions. Sorrow for the sick child warred with anger at Julee for keeping the little girl a secret from him all these years. He had never been good enough for Julee, and he hadn't been good enough to know his own daughter. The notion stabbed deep. Some perverse part of him, of the old Tate, wanted to dwell on his own pain and loss, but he fought it down. Long ago, he'd discovered that putting his own needs first always hurt him in the long run.

"Why come to me now, Julee? If I'm not a match, and there's nothing I can do to help, why are you here?"

Julee pressed a finger in the corner of each eye, and to Tate's relief, effectively stanched the trickle of tears. Seeing Julee cry had always reduced him to nothing.

She sat up straight, hunched her shoulders once as though her neck ached, then resumed perfect posture. No one had ever looked quite as elegant or as tragic as Julianna Reynolds, the hometown girl who made good, sitting at his kitchen table. Tate rose and moved around to stand behind his own chair, removing himself from the temptation of massaging Julee's tense shoulders. He knew what touching her did to his common sense, and this morning he was certain he needed every fiber of good sense he could maintain.

Because he still didn't know for sure what she wanted.

Julianna couldn't find the words. How did one ask a stranger, albeit a familiar one, to make her pregnant?

The knot of tension in her shoulders pulled tighter. Dear Lord, this was insane. She was insane. Or she would be by the time this day was over.

Wound as tightly as a new Slinky, she pushed back from the table and went to the wide double windows at the end of Tate's sunny kitchen. Outside on the green lawn, she spotted several dogs, one of them the little red mutt Tate had found the day of the bone-marrow drive. The animal had gained weight and his previously dull coat shone clean and glossy in the morning sun.

The reminder that the deeply wounded boy with the good heart had become a kind and caring man buoyed her courage.

Turning, she found him still standing behind his chair, watching her with intent green eyes. "A sibling would be the ideal bone-marrow match."

He blinked. "Does Megan have a sibling?"

"No, but if I had another baby…"

With a puzzled frown, his glance flickered to her left hand. Julianna thought she detected faint disappointment. "You said you weren't engaged."

"I'm not." The hammering in her chest grew so loud she was certain Tate could hear it. Julianna inhaled deeply, then announced on the slow exhale. "To be certain of a match, both Megan and her sibling need to have the same set of parents."

Puzzled, he opened his mouth once, closed it, then said, "But Megan's parents are you and me."

"Yes. You and me." She waited, holding her breath, while Tate absorbed the words. She knew the minute he understood because he dropped his hands and stared at her, incredulous.

"Are you saying what I think you're saying?"

Eager to convince him, she rushed to explain. "It's the only way to give Megan a chance to live a normal life. I have to have another baby. With you."

Neck muscles about to pop from the tension, Julianna thought she'd collapse on the clean beige tile. What must Tate be thinking? After nine years she'd waltzed back into his life, informed him he was a father and asked him to make her pregnant again.

Emotions played across his darkly handsome face. He looked staggered. Horrified. Bewildered. Did he think, as she was beginning to, that she was crazy?

"I wouldn't ask anything else of you," she went on desperately, afraid to let him talk, fearing his answer. "No child support. No strings. No interference whatsoever in your life." She thrust out her hands. "Please. I beg you. Just give me another baby."

"Just another baby." The way he drew the words out, clipping them off with military precision warned her that he was not taking this well. "Let me get this straight. You want us to have sex, make a baby, and then go on with our lives as though nothing had ever happened?"

Said like that, the idea sounded as cold and calculated as premeditated murder. Her hands fell to her sides.

"I only meant that I'll disrupt your life as little as possible. Once I'm pregnant I'll go back to California and resume full responsibility for the children. You won't have to do another thing."

He shook his head. "Not a chance."

Spots danced before her eyes. The room spun and she had the horrible notion that she might faint.

"You have to!" Lurching across the room, she clutched at his arm. "Megan's life depends upon it. I'll do anything, Tate. I'll even pay you. Any amount of money you ask. Whatever you want, but dear God, you can't just turn your back on her."

Tate yanked his arm away. The shuttered expression returned and the friendly, kind-hearted man disappeared, leaving her alone in the kitchen with a terrifying stranger. He glared at her, chest heaving, breathing harsh and rapid as though he'd run a marathon. A shiver of apprehension raced down her spine.

A cell phone jangled, breaking the tense silence. Julianna jumped. Pinning her with an arctic stare, Tate slapped at his belt loop and came up empty. The ring came again—from her purse. A glance down revealed her mother's cell-phone number.

Julianna reacted, ripping the flip phone from its holder on the side of her purse.

"Hello."

The voice on the other end didn't improve her morning.

"What happened?" she asked, knuckles going white on the small device. "When?"

While she spoke tersely into the mouthpiece, Tate listened, never taking his eyes off her.

What little strength she had left seeped away. She slid into the nearest chair. "I'll catch the next plane back. Tell her I love her, and I'm coming."

With a snap, she disconnected and let the phone drop into her lap, then rested her forehead on the tabletop. Dear Lord, what an absolutely abysmal day this was turning out to be.

"What's wrong? Is it Megan?"

Lifting her head, she glared at him. Why did he bother to ask when he clearly didn't care at all about his daughter?

She rubbed at the baseball-sized knot in her left shoulder. "I've got to get back to California. She's in the hospital."

"What happened?" His expression was dark and unreadable.

"She spiked a fever."

"That's bad enough to be in the hospital?"

"For a child with leukemia it can be deadly. Fever can mean infection that her weakened immune system can't fight. Or worse, that she's no longer in remission." The last thought terrified her most of all. If Megan came out of remission now, she wouldn't have a chance of survival. Julianna scraped back from the table and rose. "I've got to get back right away."

"What about our discussion?"

Incredulous, she answered, "You've made your feelings clear. You don't know Megan, and you despise me. You'll go on with your life while my little girl withers away from a disease that you have the power to stop. I hope you can live with that."

Voice harsh and unrelenting, he said, "You think you have all the answers, don't you?"

Unbidden tears welled, choking her. "I wish to God I did."

A fleeting hint of sympathy flickered in Tate's eyes. He shoved a hand across his hair. A sound of frustration issued from his throat.

Abruptly, he wheeled, going to the window where he pressed the heels of his hands into the windowsill and stared out over the sunlit backyard, shoulders hunched, back as rigid as a two-by-four. He remained that way so long that Julianna gave up hope. She slid the phone into her purse, took one last sip of lukewarm coffee and scraped back from the table.

Tate turned at the sound, his proud handsome face unreadable. Coming around the table, he spoke with surprising gentleness. "Sit down." When she only looked at him in confusion, he went on. "Drink your coffee while I make some phone calls. There's juice in the fridge if you'd prefer that."

"I need to leave."

"No." He pressed her into the chair. "Not yet."

When she looked up at him, puzzled, he dropped the bomb. "I want to meet my daughter. I'm going with you."

Chapter Six

Julianna glanced at the tense, dark male beside her and then down at his long, powerful hands gripping the armrests of the airplane seat with enough strength to rip them off. "You don't have to do this, you know."

"Yes, I do," he said in a voice that would have frozen antifreeze. After a rebellious glare reminiscent of the boy she'd known in high school he turned his back and drew the shade over the window, blocking out her words as well as the sunlit tarmac below.

Since the moment he'd nearly shocked her out of her chair with the news that he was going to California, Julianna had watched in amazement as he efficiently rearranged his life—and that of the town—in order to make the trip.

"I don't know when I'll be back," he'd said to his secretary, the woman he called Rita the Magnificent. "Jeet and Tom can handle anything that comes up."

"Yeah." His green gaze flickered up to Julee's, accusing, and her stomach did a nervous flip-flop. "A family emergency, you might say."

Just like that he'd walked away from his responsibilities in Blackwood to meet the child he hadn't known existed until this morning. His decision made no sense. If he didn't intend to help her, why was he so insistent about making this trip?

She could only pray that once he'd seen their beautiful daughter, he'd change his mind and agree to her proposal that they have another baby.

Her stomach did a double flip-flop just thinking about the implications of *that*. Sitting beside Tate McIntyre, virile and handsome, his long legs pressed against hers in the narrow space, reminded her that there was more to having a baby than being pregnant. She and Tate would have to sleep together, touch each other, make love. The knowledge brought heat to her cheeks...and a heavy yearning low in her belly. Even as angry as he was right now, Julee felt the familiar pull of physical attraction.

The little seatbelt light overhead pinged on and engines started to whine. Shifting uncomfortably, Julianna concentrated on tightening her seatbelt. Up front the attendants went through the ritual Julee had seen a thousand times.

The jet lifted off and people began to move around the cabin. Tate fell into a brooding silence, lost in his own thoughts. The rigid side angle of his face could have been cut from mocha marble. The bulge of his tight, straight jaw, the grim line of his mouth, the almost imperceptible squint of his leaf-colored eyes radiated negative emotion. Part of her understood his fury. How would she feel if the tables had been turned? Even though he had betrayed her all those years ago, the impact of what she'd asked of him, and the secret she'd kept from him was enough to unhinge any man.

The clackety-clack of the refreshment cart drew her attention. She didn't want anything, but last night's glass of airline juice was all the nutrition she'd had in two days.

"Spiced tomato juice, please, and peanuts." The protein would do her good.

"Coffee," Tate answered when the attendant turned to him. He must live on coffee the way she lived on juices.

When the cart rattled away, Julianna swished the ice around in the plastic cup. Maybe Tate could sit here like a statue all the way to California, but she couldn't.

"I haven't handled this very well, Tate. I'm sorry."

"I don't want to talk about it."

Julianna sighed, tilting her face in his direction to block out the conversations around them. "Then let's talk about Megan. You're probably wondering why I haven't told you about her before now."

"I know why." The words were more of a growl than an answer.

He knew?

She took one peanut from the shiny package and crunched thoughtfully, studying Tate's closed, forbidding expression. Did he truly know? Did he understand her devastation when she'd called his dorm room to tell him about their baby only to discover that he was no longer there? His roommate had told her about the injury, the lost scholarship, and most painful of all, about the new wife who had taken her place.

She'd known then that he'd never loved her, and from that moment, she'd closed herself off from any reminders of Blackwood and Tate McIntyre. Could he possibly understand how much he'd hurt her? Or that she'd never meant to hurt him in return?

"This may sound stupid to you, but I didn't know I was pregnant for a long time."

He dumped a package of powdered creamer into his cup, turning the coffee the color of his skin. "You're right. That's hard to believe."

"It's true. I blamed every symptom on nerves, right down to the first few times I felt her move. When I gained a little weight, I dieted like crazy, afraid I would lose my contract."

His look was condemning. "It's a wonder you didn't lose her."

"I know." He'd spoken directly to the fear that she'd done something to cause Megan's leukemia. "At first I wasn't going to tell you, but after a while, I couldn't bear not to."

His upper body twisted toward her, skepticism radiating from every pore.

"I tried to call you. I was coming home that Thanksgiving during my time off."

"Thanksgiving," he said, and some of the anger in him softened.

"Yes." She saw that he'd made the connection. He was already married by Thanksgiving.

He swallowed and turned back to his foam coffee cup. With a controlled shove, he jammed the food tray back into position and twisted uncomfortably, trying to straighten his bad knee. One hand kneaded the kneecap and Julianna fought the urge to replace his hand with hers. He'd wronged her, but in trying to do the right thing, she had hurt him, too.

Once the plane bounced down at LAX, Tate breathed a sigh of relief. Criminy, he hated flying, but he'd had to come. Julee was about to walk out on him again and this time he knew about the baby. Only this baby was nine years old.

Back home he had an agenda full enough to keep three men busy. With the election coming up at the end of the year, he needed to be campaigning, doing his job, taking care of his town. Blackwood needed him. But so did a little girl with his green eyes who might die without ever knowing her father had wanted her with all his heart.

His chest ached to think of all he'd missed. Julee had effectively shut him out for nine years, but she dang sure wasn't going to do it anymore.

"You can drop me at a nearby hotel," he said as he stowed his bag in the trunk of the taxicab. "Give me the hospital's address and I'll come over as soon as I get checked in."

"You'll stay with us. We have room." Julee leaned forward and gave the cabby an address. The gentle scent of her perfume stirred the air, mixing with the lingering concoction of human odors inside the cab.

He might be angry with her, but the thought of staying under the same roof with a woman who'd asked him to give her a baby sent his libido into overdrive. He was a man, after all, and he'd once loved Julee Reynolds enough to let her break his heart. Though he'd never give a woman that kind of power again, he broke out in a cold sweat just thinking about Julee, in the same house, wanting to have sex with him.

He pressed his head back into the cab's ratty upholstery. What was he thinking? Julee didn't want him. She wanted a stud for hire, and her offer to pay him for sex cut deep. To her he was still the kid from the wrong side of town who'd do anything for a few bucks. But he wasn't a gigolo—or a sperm donor.

Horns honked and the noise and hustle of the city set his teeth on edge. High-rise buildings made him claustrophobic. And the thick layer of smog clouding the sun would choke a horse.

What on earth was he—a country bumpkin sheriff—doing in Los Angeles with a beautiful model? Not just a model—a woman who'd had his baby and forgotten him until she needed something.

He mulled over her claim that she hadn't known she was pregnant until after he married Shelly. Even if it was true, it didn't explain why she hadn't acknowledged his knee injury or his loss of the football scholarship. He suspected the real reason for her silence. When Julee left Blackwood, she'd never intended to look back at the poor side of town.

A weight as heavy as this taxicab pressed down on him. He hadn't been this confused since he was nineteen years old.

Twisting and careening through more traffic than Tate ever wanted to see again, the cab finally pulled up in front of a glass-and-concrete hospital complex larger than the entire main street of Blackwood.

Taking the single bag he'd packed and Julee's small overnight case, he followed her across a wide driveway, through the glass double doors into the unnatural quiet of the children's hospital. That Julee had spent plenty of time here was painfully obvious. Without hesitation she led the way to a row of elevators and pushed the up button. The door pinged open. Several people came out as he and Julee boarded.

Inside they were alone. After pressing the number, Julee turned to him, nervously twisting the ring on her finger.

"I have to ask a favor of you."

He set down his suitcase, dreading what was to come. Hadn't her bizarre request for a baby been enough for one day?

"What now?"

"Megan's mental outlook is absolutely essential to her health. We have to keep her happy, upbeat. The last thing we can afford to do is upset her."

"I don't want to upset her. I just want to meet her. She's my daughter."

The elevator pinged past two floors before Julee worked up the nerve to answer. "But she doesn't know that." She twisted the ring again, preparing him for more bad news. "Megan thinks her father died before she was born."

If she'd hit him with a brick he couldn't have hurt more. All the strength drained out of his arms. Julee was so ashamed of getting pregnant by that McIntyre boy that she'd told his daughter he was dead. He felt humiliated the same way he had as a child when strangers came to his trailer with hand-me-down clothes and bags of groceries.

"This may come as a big surprise, Julee, but I'm not dead. Maybe I was to you, but I'm not to her. I'm her father. Why not tell her the truth?"

"Because it's too dangerous. Her fragile health might not stand the shock. Think what it might do to her emotional health to discover not only that her father is alive, but that her mother has lied to her all her life."

"Whose fault is that?"

"Fault isn't the issue here." Julee's eyes burned with a fanatical flame. "Megan's health is all that matters. We're fighting a life-and-death battle. Nothing and no one can interfere with our chance to win."

Grudgingly he relented. Megan's health was the important issue, not his wounded pride. "All right, then. This is your game. Tell me how to play it. Because I am going to see her. And I am going to be a part of her life, even if she thinks I'm the Easter Bunny."

"A partial truth will work best, I think. I'll introduce you as an old friend from Blackwood who knew her father."

"How will you explain my coming here like this?"

"I won't just yet. Right now she's sick. We'll think of something when the time comes."

The elevator shushed to a stop and dinged open. They stepped out and padded in strained silence down a long hall. On each side, small children lay in beds surrounded by machines that no child should even know about. The thought that his daughter was intimately acquainted with many of them broke Tate's heart all over again.

At room 1421 Julee paused, her hand on the door handle. "Will you let me go in first? Alone?"

He dropped back, left out again. "Sure." He stood there uneasily, holding both their travel bags. "What about these?"

"Mom's car is here. We'll stash them in the trunk after I check on Megan and see what's going on." She pushed the door open and disappeared inside. Almost immediately Beverly Reynolds, older than he remembered, stepped into the hallway. She didn't seem the least bit surprised to see him, an indication that Julee must have informed her of her wild idea. If he'd ever blushed in his life, he would have done so then.

"Mrs. Reynolds." She was much shorter than Julee, forcing Tate to look down.

"Tate. Hello." She gave him a worried smile. "Let's go put those bags in the car while Julee talks with the doctors."

"The doctors are in there now?"

Beverly laid a hand on his arm. "We'll come right back up."

Reluctant to leave without finally seeing his child, he followed her down into the parking garage.

By the time they returned, Julee waited for them outside the room, her back against the closed door.

"She's asleep," she said.

Disappointment seeped through Tate. "What did the doctors say?"

"She has a mild infection, thank heaven. One they can control with antibiotics."

"She'll be okay?"

"For now."

"I want to see her." At Julee's hesitation, his patience snapped. "Look, Julee," he said with quiet insistence. "I've come fifteen hundred miles to see a child I didn't know existed, and I'm not leaving here until I at least get to look at her. I'm not some rowdy boy anymore, who doesn't know how to be quiet around sick people."

"You're right. I'm sorry." Unnecessarily holding a finger to her lips, she led him into the room.

Tate's eyes strained to see his child. His heart thumped madly. He hadn't been this scared since he'd looked down the business end of a Saturday-night special. How was a man supposed to react in a situation like this?

A small, narrow form lay curled on her side beneath a sheet. Her cheek rested on one hand and dark lashes fanned flushed cheekbones. She was painfully thin and so beautiful his chest expanded with pride. Regret, sorrow, delight and pure terror ripped through him.

"She's so beautiful," he whispered in awe. "God, Julee, she's gorgeous."

An IV tube snaked beneath the sheet, dripping yellowish fluid into Megan's arm. A light flashed off and on. A small ticking sound emanated from the IV pump. He hated the thought that someone had poked a needle in those pencil-thin arms.

"She'll sleep awhile," Julee whispered, a soft, motherly expression on her face. "Why don't we go down to the cafeteria and grab a bite to eat?"

"You go. I'll sit here beside her." He wanted to look at his child, to mentally photograph every curve and angle of her face. He'd never been a father before.

"Mom will stay with her. We need to talk." She shot a warning glance at the sleeping child. "But not here."

Her meaning was obvious. They couldn't risk Megan overhearing the truth about him. Reluctantly, Tate backed away from the bed, taking one last look at his little girl before following Julee out the door and back toward the elevators.

He made it as far as the empty waiting area before the riot of emotion inside him exploded. For years, he'd kept his bad-boy temper under control, but all day long it had pushed to the front, threatening to overwhelm him. From the moment Julee had told him her well-kept secret, he'd battled a growing rage. But now, seeing the daughter he'd never known sick and possibly dying, anger, frustration and helplessness erupted. Fists clenched, he pressed his forehead against the wall.

"Why?" he asked from between teeth clenched tightly enough to break a molar. "Why does something like this have to happen to an innocent child?"

Her voice came softly from behind his shoulder. "I don't know."

"Why couldn't I have been a match? She could have had anything of mine—my blood, my arms, my heart—anything. Why couldn't I have done this simple thing for her?"

Julee laid a hand on his back. He tensed, needing her

comfort, but too wary to accept it. "Was it me? Did I cause this? Did something tainted in my bastard blood make her sick?"

"No, Tate, no. You didn't cause Megan's cancer." Gently, she tugged at his shoulder, turning him around. A pair of eyes, blue as an Oklahoma sky, begged him. "Neither of us made her sick, but together we can do something to save her."

"This is crazy. You know it and so do I." He couldn't believe he was actually considering such a thing, but now that he'd seen his only child, he desperately wanted to know her. And how would that be possible if leukemia took her life?

"I don't know what else to do." Julee rubbed at the tension in her shoulders. "Do you?"

He banged his clenched fists together. "No."

"Does that mean…?" Hope flared on Julee's face and Tate fought the urge to hold her. If he did this totally irrational thing, he'd be putting his heart, not to mention his soul, in jeopardy.

"Let's get something straight, Julee. I'm not for hire. I don't want your danged money, but I do want to know my daughter, and I'll do everything in my power to make her well, even something as crazy as making another baby."

"You won't regret this, I promise."

He raised a palm. "Wait. I'm not finished."

She paused, uncertain.

"All my life I lived under the shadow of never having a father. That hurts a child, Julee. It cuts into the very center of a kid's self-worth. Megan should have known me. She should have had my name."

"But you can't tell her! It's too dangerous."

He chopped the air impatiently. "I can't change the

choices you made for Megan, but I will not intentionally father a child to grow up a bastard like I did.''

''But I thought…''

''You thought what? That I'd make you pregnant and disappear for another ten years?'' He shook his head. ''Not a chance. If we're going to have a baby together, we're going to do it right.''

''I don't understand.''

''Let me spell it out for you, then. Kids deserve a mother and a daddy. The only way I'll father another baby is if that child bears my name legally. You and I will have to get married.''

Julee's left hand, glittering with a gem he'd never be able to afford, clutched at her throat. ''Married!''

Her horrified reaction made him unintentionally gruff.

''That's the deal. Take it or leave it. If you want another child, you'll have to marry me.''

Chapter Seven

Julianna hadn't even thought twice before agreeing to marry Tate. When she'd said she'd do anything to save Megan, she'd meant it. Even Megan had taken the news in her usual stride, buying the story that her mom and Tate had fallen in love at "second sight." And to Tate's credit he'd charmed his daughter into agreeing that he was the best thing since Super Nintendo.

"Julee, this little girl is prettier than Miss America," he'd said as they stood beside the hospital bed, Megan's feverish face gazing at them curiously. Julianna knew he must be anxious, meeting his daughter for the first time under such bizarre circumstances, but he was as cool as mountain air.

Megan smiled at his compliment, and the sun came out for Julianna. "Are you really going to marry my mom?"

"That's the plan. The sooner the better." Tate slid an arm around Julianna's waist, surprising her with his display of affection. He was really turning on the charm for Megan's sake, and for that she was grateful. Never mind that her body reacted wildly to his touch. Given the circumstances and the fact that she had asked him to sleep with her tonight, a certain amount of anticipatory interest was to be expected.

"Mama says the town thinks you're a superhero."

Tate laughed. "Yeah, that's me. Super Sheriff. Want to see me fly?" Releasing his hold on Julianna, he flapped his arms like chicken wings.

Megan giggled. "You're funny." She glanced at her mother. "Did you really go to high school with Super Sheriff?"

"Yes. But he was a football player then, not a sheriff."

"I bet you were a super football player, too."

An odd look crossed Tate's face, and Julianna's heart went out to him. "Not super enough, I guess. Messed up my knee and had to stop playing."

The essence of sympathy, Megan patted his hand with her own, the IV tube restricting her reach. "It stinks pretty bad when you have to stop doing something because you get sick."

"Yeah. But I like being sheriff, and we're going to get you well, so you can do anything you please."

And so the announcement had gone. Easier than they'd expected.

The hard part had come two hours later as she and Tate stood before the justice of the peace reciting the age-old vows. Stiffening her spine, she'd fought down the nervous churning in her belly, her heart thumping erratically at the notion of marriage to the tall, handsome stranger beside her.

Looking gorgeous in a white golf shirt and chinos, he'd been as stiff and nervous as she, clearing his throat several times before agreeing to take her as his wife.

Afterward, as they signed the wedding certificate, he'd offered to take her out to dinner but she'd refused.

"That's not necessary, Tate," she'd said. "Our marriage isn't for keeps or for love, and those are the reasons to celebrate."

The idea of a marriage that would last only until a new baby was born didn't appeal, but that was the deal they'd made. Once the baby came and Megan had her transplant, they would divorce so each could go on with their separate lives as before. So sad to plan a divorce on the same day of the wedding, but neither carried any delusions into the agreement. They were marrying for Megan, not for each other.

So in the end, they'd stopped back at the hospital and stayed until Megan fell asleep, a smile on her sweet face at the news of her Mom's marriage. Julianna knew an older child would have questioned the speed of the marriage, but to a third-grader, today was the only day that counted.

With her mother tactfully remaining at the hospital with Megan, Tate and Julianna had gone home to the condo. It was late, and both were too keyed up to eat and too tired to sleep. A good thing she supposed, since this was their wedding night and they had married for the express purpose of making love.

Heat pooled in her belly while a shiver of nerves skittered up the back of her neck. Making love with Tate again after all these years both terrified and titillated.

They'd clicked on the TV, but neither watched it. Tate prowled around the condo like a caged panther, staring out the window, saying little. The time came when she could no longer put off the inevitable. Rising from the flowered couch, she said, "I think I'll take a shower and go to bed."

Tate spun away from the window, expression unreadable. "Go ahead. I'll be in shortly."

He'd tactfully waited to take his own shower until she lay between the fresh-scented sheets of her queen-size bed.

Throat dry, Julianna listened to the unfamiliar sounds of a man in her bathroom. Not just any man. Her husband. Dear heavens, when this wild idea of having another baby had come to her, she certainly hadn't planned on marriage, hadn't even considered such a crazy option. But then all her options lately had been crazy.

Tate came out of the bathroom, a tall shadow with the light at his back. His hesitant stance said he, too, was nervous about this wedding night. When he moved forward, toward the bed, her heart banged wildly against her rib cage. He wore only boxers. The well-honed muscles of his chest and arms and legs rippled as he sat down on his side of the bed. His dark hair glistened damply in the faint glow of the outside security lights.

Repressing the urge to skitter to the far edge of the bed and too embarrassed to stare at his incredible body, Julianna lay as stiff as a dead fish and trained her gaze on the shadows dancing across the ceiling.

"Are you okay?" His gravelly voice made her shiver.

Suddenly short of breath, she nodded. "I'm sorry. This is so awkward."

"Yeah."

He lifted the sheets and slid beneath, releasing a warm, damp shower scent that toyed with her senses and struck her anew with the enormity of what they were doing.

"I don't know if I can go through with this."

He rolled toward her. One dark, muscled forearm, sprinkled with black hair, molded the sheet to his belly. His powerful chest and shoulders extended above the covers. "A heck of a time to decide that, don't you think?"

She swallowed hard, the sound loud in the quiet darkness. "What if this is a sin, Tate? Is it wrong to love my child so desperately? Is it immoral to have another baby this way?" Words tumbled out, half-baked thoughts, fears, worries. "I never meant to do anything wrong. I only want to—"

He listened patiently while she talked herself empty. When he spoke, his quiet sympathy soothed her. "We've both made our share of mistakes. Trying to save our daughter isn't one of them."

She breathed a deep, shivering sigh. "You're right. Our feelings aren't important. Megan is all that matters."

Some of the stiffness eased. The bed tilted and Tate's large, athletic body shifted toward her. The anxious knot bloomed in her belly.

"Tate?"

"Yeah?" His voice rumbled close to her ear. They'd never been in a bed together.

"Could we wait until— I mean— Today has been so hectic and it's really late," she finished lamely.

She tried to see him, tried to read his face in the dark room, the sculpted angle of his cheekbones, the high thrust of his shoulder above the sheet. She could feel him, smell his clean soapy scent, but she couldn't read him.

"You're calling the shots."

Relieved, yet oddly disappointed, Julianna rolled onto her side, back to her new husband, and closed her eyes. Her insides shook as if an earthquake had struck. How was she ever going to pull this off?

Tate lay in the darkness for a long time listening to the hushed flow of the air-conditioning system and watching shadows play across the ceiling. A deep heaviness weighed him down.

Even now, when she needed him—when Megan needed him—Julee couldn't stand to let that trashy McIntyre boy touch her. He felt helpless, out of control, the way he'd felt ten years ago.

He wanted to be angry—angry because of the secret she'd kept. Angry because the daughter he'd never known suffered from a horrible disease. Angry because this marriage to Julianna Reynolds gave her the power to destroy him again. But he wasn't angry. He was hurt, his heart throbbing as if it had been pounded with a tire tool.

Nothing in law enforcement prepared a man for this.

Impatient with his scattered thoughts, he flopped over, then regretted the move. Accustomed to sleeping alone, his large body created a tidal wave that jarred Julee. She stirred, and the soft mewing that emanated from her sleeping form titillated him. His body reacted.

She was right here beside him. With very little effort, he could touch her, feel the soft silk of those long legs against his. Wasn't that what this impromptu marriage was all about?

Maybe. But Julee was calling the shots. Until she wanted him, he wouldn't push the matter.

Quietly, letting Julee get the rest her exhausted body needed, he eased from beneath the sheet. His knee caught and he grabbed for it, setting the bed atremble. After a pause, he rose, heard the exaggerated groan of the innersprings, and glanced down at Julee. When she remained still, he crept away, going to the window.

The sweep of car lights reminded him where he was. The country boy in him yearned for home, for the thump of his dogs on the front porch, and the howl of an occasional coyote. Though Julee lived in an exclusive neighborhood, it was still a crowded city, houses and condos stacked on top of one another.

Like an elephant in a glass factory, that was him. So out of place.

He didn't know how long he stood there, staring at the brick façade of the next condo, thinking, wondering how this would all turn out. He was lost in thought when Julee's soft voice came to him.

"Tate. Are you okay?"

Turning, he saw she'd raised up on one elbow, her hair slightly mussed and incredibly sexy. This time he didn't fight the kick of attraction.

"Sure. You?" He was anything but okay, but he had agreed to this insanity. Why worry her with his tumultuous thoughts?

"Twenty-four hours ago you didn't even know you had a daughter. And now you're married to someone you hardly know. You must be reeling from the shock."

Drawn by the soft regret in her tone, Tate moved to the bedside. He looked down at his beautiful wife, warm and flower-scented. Criminy! Julianna Reynolds was his wife! Ten years ago he would have killed for this moment.

"My last twenty-four hours can't compare to the nightmare you've lived with for months."

Looking up with a bemused expression, Julee surprised him by scooting aside to make room on the edge of the bed. Lifting a hand, she gestured him down. When he'd sat, she laid her elegant fingers along his forearm. Reflexively, his muscles tensed.

Julee smiled gently. "I won't bite."

He grinned back. "Maybe you should."

Cocooned by the intimacy of darkness, they both relaxed, letting down long-erected defenses.

"Tell me about her," Tate said.

"What do you want to know?"

"Anything. Everything. What does she like? What's she good at? What's her favorite food?"

"She's a typical nine-year-old in most ways. She can

be incredibly funny and silly. She giggles and writes in her diary. She likes pizza and Roller-Blading and slumber parties. She's much better at math than I'll ever be.''

''You always hated math.''

Julee faked a shudder. ''I'd never have passed if you hadn't tutored me.''

He'd barely passed himself, but not because he couldn't do the work. Back then, he hadn't seen the point, so he'd cut more classes than he'd made. Fortunately, showing up on test days had saved his tail and kept him eligible to play football.

''And,'' Julee's soft, sexy voice went on, ''she can draw anything, just like her father.''

A curl of pleasure rose in Tate's chest. ''She likes to draw?''

''She's good, too. Just like you. I'll show you some of her pictures in the morning.''

He hadn't drawn anything but his weapon in years, though in high school, art had been a way to communicate all the torment inside him. He hadn't realized that then, but the years in law enforcement had taught him a lot about human psychology.

''Remember that time you entered one of my drawings in an art contest?''

''You were so ticked off.''

''Until they handed me that fifty bucks.'' He hadn't wanted anyone but Julee to see inside him that way.

She laughed softly. ''That did ease the pain a little, didn't it?''

''Yeah.''

''Then you spent every penny on me.'' The hand on his arm began to stroke tiny circles. Electric sparks shot out from Julee's fingers, sensitizing the hairs on his arm.

''Not every penny. I gave Mama ten bucks for bingo.''

"I still have that necklace."

"You're kidding."

"No." The long fingernails lightly scraped downward, raising every nerve ending on the way to his hand. Soft and smooth, like warm velvet, her fingers curled into his.

Tate's heart began a steady drumming. If she wanted to seduce him, she wasn't going to have to work very hard. He'd been too busy for too long and nothing sounded quite as wonderful as making sweet love to Julianna Reynolds. With a jolt, he amended the thought. Julianna McIntyre.

"Why don't you come back to bed?" she whispered.

Denoting a hint of nervousness, Tate twisted around to face her, bringing his bare thighs alongside her body. He knew what she was asking. Wasn't this why they'd married? To make love? To make a baby?

A baby. A living, breathing combination of Julee and himself. Maybe a boy who liked football. Or another little girl with elm-leaf eyes. Responsibility pounded at him. He struggled with the ethics, but lost the battle when Julee sat up. The sheet fell away as she leaned forward to run her hand over his shoulder.

He'd been wanting to touch her, really touch her, since the day she'd stormed into Blackwood demanding his blood and his assistance.

Stilling the tremble in his fingers, he brushed the mussed hair back from her face. She was painted in shades of dark and light, though he knew the blue of her eyes, the rose tint of her mouth, the pearl of her skin. Hadn't he seen them a thousand times in his tormented dreams?

She wrapped one slim arm over his and held his hand against her cheek. He could feel the corner of her mouth, soft and moist, against his palm. Slowly, he leaned in, easing her back onto the pillow. He followed her down, watching her eyes, gauging her reaction, waiting for the sign that this was what she wanted. When she slid both hands along his shoulders and into the hair at the back of his neck, lips parted in welcome, he stifled a groan.

Somehow he'd have to make love to his wife while still guarding his heart. How would he manage such a thing when Julee's soft womanly body gave beneath his so perfectly and the history between them magically throbbed to life again with every movement?

When his lips touched hers, he almost changed his mind. Julee was a sweet, dangerous abyss. If he fell in again, he'd never survive. He removed his lips from hers and found her velvet cheek, fighting down the panic—and the soaring need.

"Tate," Julee whispered, her breath moist and sweet against his ear. "Kiss me like you used to."

The lurch of passion hit him with the force of a .357 magnum. He moved his mouth back to hers, gentle at first, exploring, questioning. The flowery scent of her, the minty taste of her sweet lips, the softness of her skin overloaded his heightened senses.

Carefully, protectively, he held himself in check. But when Julee responded, touching her tongue to his in a seductive feather dance, his brain short-circuited.

He couldn't think of anything except Julee. The silken legs entwined with his, the velvet hands stroking his back, his chest, his hair, his arms. She touched him everywhere and he returned the favor, revisiting places long neglected but never forgotten. Her soft unintelligible murmurs drove him crazy. He was spinning out of control, losing himself.

Sinking, sinking, sinking. He fought against the under tow, like a man drowning in a whirlpool. Desperately, he tried to hold something back, to keep some part of him detached from the powerful source of pain and pleasure that was Julee.

But in the end, with his heart lying over hers, beating to the same wild rhythm, he shattered into a million pieces. In his mind's eye he saw the explosion—like a white-hot star, silvery bits of himself cascaded in a free fall through space and time.

While his breathing returned to normal and the sweat—both his and hers—evaporated from his body, he tenderly pulled Julee into the crook of his shoulder, holding her close to his side.

Julee laid a hand on his chest. He rolled his head to look at her and his heart seized up at the dewy, satisfied expression. She'd always looked like that afterward, and he'd felt as he did now—like the sexiest man alive.

"Thank you," she murmured. "For making this so much easier."

The words were cold water to his warm thoughts, a reminder of why she'd made love with him. Not for his sake. Or even hers. But for the sake of their child.

The knowledge hurt more now than it had before, but he set his mind to accept it. His own emotional torment had no place in this marriage, and he'd best get used to it. She was using him. A means to an end. A worthy, noble end that he agreed with wholeheartedly, but, now that he'd loved her, he had to live with one clear fact. Julianna would always be too much for him. And he would never be enough.

Julianna awakened, relaxed and rested. Stretching languidly, she smiled, remembering. Yesterday, she had married Tate McIntyre. And last night… A curl of desire stirred in her belly as she relived the gentle, tender moments in Tate's arms. She'd been scared to death, but Tate had made everything seem so natural, so right.

"Morning." Dark and delectable, he entered the bedroom, carrying a tall glass of orange juice. To her disappointment he was already fully dressed.

A warm flush suffused her. Here she lay fantasizing about a morning spent in bed, but from the looks of his neatly groomed businesslike appearance, making love again was the last thing on his mind.

She sat up and the sheet slid down, revealing what she'd forgotten. Grabbing at the cover she yanked it up again to cover her nakedness.

Tate stopped in midstride and politely averted his eyes, an action that embarrassed her even more. He'd been the one to remove her gown, but here in the light of day he couldn't look at her. Her mellow mood evaporated.

"All right. I'm decent," she said, disgruntled. Her hair was a tangled mess, thanks again to Tate. She swiped uselessly at it.

Reserved and quiet, he handed her the juice.

"Thanks."

She wanted him to sit down on the bed again and talk to her, to return to that sweet, nostalgic mood they'd shared last night. Instead, he stood a foot away, one hand thrust into his pants pocket.

"I hope you don't mind. I used your telephone."

Her mood dropped a little lower. He was her husband, no matter how temporary. And they'd slept together, for heaven's sake. He could use her phone without permission if he wanted to.

"Of course. Anytime." The words sounded stiff and formal. What was happening?

"I called the hospital. Your mom said Megan had a good night, her fever is down, and the lab has already been in to draw blood. If everything looks okay she can come home this afternoon."

"You've been busy." This time she sounded resentful.

Darn it. This wasn't the way she'd wanted their morning to go.

"I called my office, too." He shifted uneasily and if her mood could have tumbled lower, it would have. She knew she wasn't going to like what he had to say. "I really need to get back to Blackwood."

One day married, and he couldn't wait to leave her. To her dismay, the notion hurt. Didn't he remember that she could never be a one-night-stand kind of girl?

"What about our agreement? How can I get pregnant if we aren't together?"

"In the mad rush of the moment we didn't think things out too well, did we?"

They had discussed the marriage and the inevitable divorce, but they hadn't considered where they would live for the next year. Her life was here in California and his was in Oklahoma.

She sipped the tartly sweet orange juice, then set the glass on the bedside table. "Is there any way you'd consider moving here until I get pregnant?"

"No." His thunderous expression closed that option instantly.

"Okay." She blew a sigh at the wisps of hair clouding her vision. "Asking that was unfair of me, but our lives are here. And so is my career. I can't walk away from that."

"It's always been about your career, hasn't it?"

His mild disdain raised her defenses. "Not now. It's about Megan."

Surely he understood how frightened she was of losing her only means of supporting Megan. He knew her past. Knew she had no other training. Megan's needs had to come first.

His shoulders relaxed and he came to the bed, easing

down beside her, though careful to keep his body from making contact with hers. His fresh-shaved scent stirred her libido. Itching to touch him, to bring back last night's Tate, she clasped the sheet to her throat, instead.

"Could you commute?" he asked. "Come to Black-wood a couple of times a month?"

Julianna shook her head. "That might take too long. The more times we…" Biting her lip, she glanced away. The warm flush crept over her again. Last night, they'd made passionate love in this bed and this morning she couldn't even say the words. "I have to get pregnant as quickly as possible."

Tate rose and stalked to the window, hands thrust deeply into his pockets. "I know. We'll have to live together, at least for a while, whether we like it or not."

His tone hurt. The altruistic sheriff had only agreed to this marriage because of Megan, a fact that had been fine with Julianna yesterday. But last night in his arms something had happened. Something both beautiful and frightening—and totally unacceptable. She had to remember that Tate had never loved her. For Megan's sake, and for her own, she'd ignore the confused emotions swirling inside her.

She reached for the orange juice and took a second sip. The acid juice burned going down.

Though she hadn't wanted to consider the possibility, there was another way for them to be together. She'd sworn never to live in that nosy, one-horse town again, but hadn't she said she'd do anything?

Before she lost her resolve, Julee sucked in a deep breath and said, "All right then. Megan and I will move to Oklahoma."

Tate stopped dead-still. His jaw dropped. "You'd do that?"

"I'll do whatever I have to." Fear niggled at the edge of her mind. If she moved away from California, even temporarily, how would she work? How would she pay the bills?

"What about Megan's health care? Doesn't she need to be here with the doctors who know her?"

"Actually, Oklahoma could be the best possible place for her transplant." At Tate's arched eyebrow, she explained, "According to Megan's oncologist, some highly touted physician at the Oklahoma Medical Center recently received a grant to do stem-cell research."

He frowned. "Stem-cell research? What does that have to do with Megan?"

Tate came toward her then, head tilted in that questioning way she'd seen last night right before he'd kissed her. Annoyed at her train of thought, Julianna took refuge in her juice glass. Reminders of her wedding night did not belong in this stilted conversation. Not when she was about to risk everything.

Fortified, she placed the glass on the nightstand and repeated the parts of Dr. Padinsky's explanation that she'd understood. "One part of stem-cell research is the use of cord blood instead of bone marrow for transplants. The procedure is still experimental, but the success rate between siblings is extremely high. When I asked the oncologist for his advice on having another child for Megan's sake he told me about stem cells. They always match. The tricky part is waiting to see if Megan's weakened system will adequately reproduce those cells."

"You discussed this with Megan's doctor? Before you came to me?"

"I'd only heard about this kind of thing, Tate. I had no idea if it would apply to Megan until I discussed the possibility with her doctors."

"And you knew all along I'd agree to have another baby." He said the words flatly, his jaw tight, as though she'd cheated him somehow.

"Of course not. But once the idea came to me I had to investigate every possible aspect."

Like a restless panther he moved from the bed to the window, then from the window to the dresser where he picked up a picture of Megan and stared down for a long time.

Julianna's heart twisted. She'd put him in a terrible position, and though he could hardly bear to look at her in the light of day, his innate decency wouldn't let him ignore the needs of his child.

"So, you'd be willing to move with Megan to Blackwood for the next year?"

"If I have to."

"What about modeling? Are you just going to leave that?"

"Of course not! Not permanently anyway." In the modeling business, out of sight meant out of mind—an unnerving prospect. But if she had to leave L.A.—and her modeling career—to save her daughter's life, she'd do it.

"What if Megan doesn't want to move?"

"Megan is nine years old. To her this will be an adventure, a chance to meet new friends in a new school, a vacation to the country." And for Julianna it would be walking into a nightmare. Back to the town she'd wanted to escape and the man who'd broken her heart.

"A vacation." Gently replacing the photograph he moved toward the doorway, pulling his reserve around him like a robe. "I guess you have everything figured out, then, don't you?"

No, not quite everything. She didn't know how she'd manage to maintain her career and meet her pressing financial obligations. Nor had she figured out how in the world she could make another baby with this gorgeous, enigmatic man, then return to California as if nothing had ever happened.

Chapter Eight

All of Blackwood was abuzz with the news of Sheriff McIntyre's unexpected sudden marriage to Julianna Reynolds. Rumor said they'd never gotten over their teenage love and had rekindled that love during the bone-marrow drive. The sheriff's unprecedented trip to California proved this theory. Everyone knew the sheriff hated to fly, and only a man madly in love would ignore so great a fear in pursuit of his one true love. Furthermore, Tate never took a day off and he'd taken two!

Some even speculated that Julee's child belonged to Tate, but that notion was too preposterous to gain much ground when the marriage itself was such a delicious topic. The gossips loved it. The old ladies tittered and sighed. And a few young ladies were downright mad.

Tate, long accustomed to being the subject of someone's gossip, blew it off as he caught up on his work and waited anxiously for his new family to arrive from California. Five days had passed since he'd left them. Tormented with dreams of his mind-altering wedding night, he'd taken over the midnight-to-seven shift. He couldn't sleep anyway. Might as well be working.

When the unfamiliar car pulled into his driveway just after noon, Tate's pulse kicked up a notch. They were here.

As casually as he knew how, he stepped out onto the porch and watched his wife and daughter climb out of the blue sedan. A spark of excitement, unlike anything he'd ever experienced, kindled inside him. He reined in the aberrant thought that they were his real family coming home after a long trip.

Julee, looking like a sunflower in a yellow outfit with her long brown hair billowing around her shoulders, glanced up and smiled. "Hello."

"Hi." Awkward as a schoolboy, Tate started down the steps, unable to take his eyes off her. Julee seemed at a loss for words, too, for she only stood there, smiling softly, her gaze holding his. Criminy, seeing her felt right. Tempted to haul her into his arms and kiss her senseless, he gripped the porch post and waited.

"Will they bite me?"

Both adults turned at the small voice. Megan, surrounded by several exuberant dogs, waited tentatively beside the car.

"Only if you're a T-bone steak," Tate answered and was rewarded with a giggle. His stomach did a funny flip-flop. Megan, a Dodgers' cap covering her short brown hair, went down on her knees and threw both arms around the largest, hairiest, ugliest dog on the place. A smaller dog, jealous of the attention, nosed his way beneath Megan's arms, knocking her over.

"Hey, you two big jerks." Sorry to leave the warmth of Julee's smile, but eager to make his child feel at home, Tate marched to the car and lifted the laughing Megan to her feet. "How ya doing, Miss America?"

She returned his banter. "Hi, Super Sheriff. I like your dogs. We don't have a dog." Swiping a hand across the back of her hot-pink shorts, she looked around. "I like your house, too. You sure have a lot of land. Do you have cows and horses and stuff like that?"

"Nope. But if you want some, I'll get them."

"Tate," Julee admonished. "Don't promise her things like that."

"Why not?"

"Because."

His heart sank at the subtle message. They wouldn't be here forever and Julee didn't want Megan getting attached to animals she couldn't take back to California.

And Julee. Lord, after sleeping with her once he was a basket case. How was he going to feel a year from now?

"How was your flight?" he asked, pushing dogs aside as he helped Julee haul luggage from the trunk of the car.

"The best kind. Uneventful."

Clomping up the steps he led the way into the house, anxious that his modest home pass muster, but annoyed that he cared.

She sniffed the air appreciatively. "Someone's been cleaning."

"Air freshener." Except for an occasional "power cleaning" by a local maid service, he cleaned his own house. Yesterday he'd opted for the power cleaning.

Megan skipped past them, a shepherd mix lumbering after her. "Where's my room?"

"Down that hall." He followed with her luggage, stopping along the way to push open a door. "Bathroom's right here."

"Cool." She peeked inside, then bounced on to the indicated bedroom. Julee followed, gazing curiously into each room.

"Do you let the dogs in the house?"

"Guess I do now."

Still wearing her ever-present smile and baseball cap, Megan glanced around the white-walled bedroom, then flopped backward onto the bed. The stubs of her short dark hair stuck out around her ears. The shepherd sat at the end of the bed, tail thumping. "This comforter is really pretty. Do you guys sleep in the room next door?"

The question was a simple one but the heat of embarrassment rose under Tate's collar. Julee turned away, walking to the window where she raised the blinds and peered out.

"My room's at the other end of the house. Closer to the garage in case I get called out at night." He didn't know why he felt the need to explain. He'd always slept there.

But in truth, a bedroom at the opposite end of the house from a curious child made an uncomfortable situation that much more tolerable.

"Would you like something to drink?" he asked, eager to change the subject. "I have tea and lemonade and all kinds of pop. There's juice too if you want it. Apple, orange, grape."

Julee turned back to him, amused. "Is that all you have to offer us poor thirsty travelers?"

He quirked an eyebrow. "Did I overdo it?"

"Yes, but you've succeeded in making us feel welcome. Thank you."

"What do you plan to do about the rental car?"

"It's a leased vehicle, not a rental. Since Mom is keeping mine in L.A. I'll need something to drive while we're here."

Another reminder of their temporary arrangement. "Your mother doesn't have a car?"

"We've always shared one to save on expenses. With

me gone and the condo to keep up, Mom is looking into a part-time job. She'll need the transportation.''

Her reply puzzled him. A famous model worried about expenses?

"With the leased car," she went on, "you won't have to taxi us back and forth to Megan's doctor's visits.''

"I wouldn't mind that." In fact, he'd planned on going. He had nine years to make up for.

"You have your own life. We'll try our best not to impose.''

"How could spending time with my family be an imposition?''

"Don't do that, Tate," she said, low enough that Megan couldn't hear. But he understood her meaning. She'd arrived five minutes ago and already she was thinking about leaving. Like the day they'd gotten married. Married and divorced, all in one day. Oh, he'd have all the visitation rights he wanted and she'd even tell Megan he was her father once the transplant was successfully done. But in the end, she'd still go back to California, back to her fancy career and her fancy life. And she'd take his children with her.

Julianna had been nervous as a cat about seeing Tate again, but he'd seemed genuinely pleased to see them. Megan, she supposed, was the reason. He made no secret of his fascination with his new daughter. After their last strained day in California, she was certainly not the cause of his friendliness.

"Mama. Mama!" Megan burst through the back door, eyes shining. "There's this really cool thing out here. You gotta come see.''

Julianna allowed her child to pull her out the back door. Tate followed. A covered porch lined the side of the house for ten feet or so. A couple of lawn chairs, an outdoor grill, and several large buckets of dog food dotted the wooden porch.

In a giant oak tree behind the house a tire swing hung from a thick rope. While Tate and Julianna stopped on the porch, Megan ran to the swing, climbed inside and pushed off.

"I've never seen her so excited."

Tate frowned. "Getting excited won't hurt her, will it?"

"No, this is wonderful. As long as she's in remission she can do whatever she pleases."

"Good." He motioned to a lawn chair, then sat down in the one opposite hers. "I tilled up a spot on the south side of the house in case she wants to make her own little garden. Planting time comes soon, and I figured she doesn't get a chance to do much of that in the city."

"What a thoughtful thing to do." Today Tate was showing her his sweet side. If he kept this up, spending a year away from her home, her mom and her job would be much easier. And leaving would be much harder. "Megan will love that."

And so would she. The potted plants around her pool were as close to gardening as she'd been in years.

Tate shrugged, but his expression was pleased. "Most kids like to grow things."

"How do you know so much about kids?"

"Youth groups, Little League, church, that sort of thing. As sheriff I like to get involved. Teaching kids productive use of their time makes my job easier in the long run."

"You should know." At the reminder of what a hellion he'd been she clapped her hand over her lips. "I'm sorry. That was rude."

She glanced up, worried she'd offended him. Green eyes danced with mischief above a wide grin.

"That's what makes me a good lawman." He pumped his eyebrows. "I know all the tricks."

The ubiquitous dogs had found them and wandered around the porch sniffing pant legs and each other.

Julianna shook her head. "Do you really keep all the stray dogs in town?"

"Nah. I eventually find homes for most of them." His hand rested on one shaggy head. "This one's Satellite. And that one making a nuisance of himself is Junkyard. You met him the day of the parade."

The little red dog licked her ankles. With a giggle, she lifted Junkyard onto her lap and rubbed his ears.

"You give them all names?"

"Even a stray deserves a name."

"So, who's this big fellow?" A floppy-eared hound stuck his head beneath the arms of the lawn chair. Julee rewarded his efforts with a pat.

"That's Burger."

"Burger? Junkyard? Satellite? Where did you get such unique names?"

"Name 'em after the place I find 'em usually. Helps me remember. For instance, I found Burger behind Johnson's Hamburger Barn. Picked Junkyard up at the salvage outside town."

"I get it. And Satellite?"

"Someone abandoned one of those huge old satellite dishes and when a storm knocked it over, Satellite was trapped underneath."

"Ah." A rangy bird dog with his tail tucked between his legs belly-crawled toward them. "Who's this anxious fellow?"

"Pitstop."

Julianna raised an eyebrow and received Tate's wicked

grin in return. "One night on a country road I stopped to—uh—you know."

"Oh," she said, immediately understanding. "You had to go...?"

"Yeah, I had to go."

She couldn't hold back the giggle bubbling inside. "Pitstop. That's too funny."

He laughed with her and in the next instant they both were laughing all out of proportion to the joke.

"Come on." Grabbing her hand, he pulled her from the chair. "I want to show you something."

Feeling like a giddy teenager, Julee tripped along behind him, hurrying to keep up with his long stride.

They left Megan swinging in the tire. No less than four dogs lay on their bellies watching her with adoring expressions. Each time she swung close enough, she dragged a sandaled foot across a furry back. Tails thumped in rhythm to the back rubs.

Hand tingling from the warm grip of Tate's fingers, Julee allowed herself to be guided toward a large outbuilding.

"Is that the barn?"

"Sort of."

"What's in there?"

"You'll see," he said mysteriously, and the tingle in her hand spread to her chest. Being with Tate had been like that in high school—exhilarating, exciting and she'd never known what to expect out of him. Though he was far more grown-up and responsible, he was no less dangerous.

She had to be here for a year. Though good sense said she should keep a distance, such a thing was impossible under the circumstances. Might as well enjoy what she could. Regardless of Tate's ability to withdraw into him-

self in moody reticence, he was an easy man to enjoy—
as long as she didn't enjoy him too much.

At the barn's entrance, he stopped. A long wooden latch
lay across the heavy door. To open it, he dropped her hand.
A wave of inexplicable loneliness shifted over her.

With a scraping sound of wood against wood the door
slid back to reveal a dark, cavernous interior. Entering behind Tate, her eyes adjusted.

Tate crossed to an electrical box, opened it and flipped
a lever. Bright fluorescent light bathed the building.

"There. Now we can see."

Julianna gazed around curiously at the combination stor-
age shed and workshop, the kind of place her father had
tinkered in when she was a child. Tools hung from a peg-
board above a long workbench. A red lawnmower and
some garden tools rested in one corner. In the center of
everything was a large tarp-covered vehicle of some sort.

"What's that?" She moved toward it, but Tate stepped
in front of her blocking the way. Standing chest to chest
she looked into his eyes, heart skidding crazily. A half
smile, full of some emotion that made her spine tingle and
her breathing short, lifted one side of his lips. What was
going on here?

A hint of his woodsy cologne mixed with the oily me-
chanical scent of the building. "Close your eyes."

Feeling silly, but incredibly young and carefree, Julianna complied. She heard the swoosh of the tarp sliding
away.

"Okay. You can look."

She opened her eyes to find Tate leaning against the
front fender of an old truck, legs crossed at his ankles,
hands tucked into his armpits, looking like the cat that ate
the canary.

With a jolt, she recognized the truck.

"You still have this?" she asked, incredulous.

"Couldn't give it up. Eventually I want to restore it to the original. Right now I only have time to work on it when my buddy from the Big Brothers program comes out. It's our project."

"You've painted it." She ran her fingers over the glossy red metal, recalling the rust and faded red of years gone by. "Does the door still stick?"

"Yep." Grinning, he wrenched the door open with a hollow scrape of metal. "Hop in."

As Julianna hauled herself onto the black-and-gray tweed seats, an avalanche of memories tumbled in. "We drove a million miles in this old truck."

"I wasn't sure if you would remember." Tate stood inside the open door, elbow propped on the roof. "Movies, ball games…" He arched an eyebrow. "The old highway."

Their favorite parking spot. They'd been so young then, so foolish, not recognizing the impossible. And even though she was a grown woman now and worldly wise, the memory of all they'd done in this old truck started a bongo beat in her chest. Attempting to keep her emotions in check and maintain a lighthearted atmosphere, she punched his arm.

With barely a flinch, Tate laughed. "The old highway was my favorite."

Julianna returned his smile, thinking how devastatingly handsome he looked in snug blue jeans and a yellow T-shirt, his teeth flashing white against dark skin.

Here on his own turf, Tate was funny and warm and full of nostalgia. After the strain of L.A., here, at least, they could use their past to establish some common ground.

"Does the stereo still work?" Leaning forward, she fiddled with the radio, poking at the cassette's Eject button.

"Yeah, but it only plays oldies," he said facetiously. "Like this one."

Using his index fingers he began a drum beat on the roof of the truck and worked his way down the window, to the hood, singing the old M.C. Hammer tune. "Can't touch this. Dah-da-da-da."

Julianna watched curiously through the windshield while Tate, looking young and relaxed, tapped out the familiar rhythm. Where was the stiff military sheriff who'd resisted her efforts for the bone-marrow drive? Where was the cool customer who'd slept with her, handed her some orange juice and walked away?

"And especially this one." Strutting around the front of the pickup, he launched into a version of "I'm too Sexy." As he flexed his arms in mock body-builder style, they both laughed.

Enjoying herself more than she'd expected, Julianna climbed out to join him, sashaying around the truck in a silly dance as he called up one favorite tune after another.

"And what about this one?" she said, recalling her own oldies flashback. "I-yi-will always love you—oo."

"Hey." Tate stopped in midstrut, the silliness seeping away. His handsome face grew serious. "That was our song."

Julianna could have stuffed a dirty sock in her mouth. Why had she chosen that particular song? She wanted them both to be comfortable with this arranged marriage, but she had no desire to relive the bittersweet time that had broken her into a million pieces.

Before she realized Tate's intent, he'd pulled her into his arms in a slow dance, softly singing the love song against her ear. His warm breath tickled the hair above her ears and raised goose bumps up and down the sensitive flesh of her neck.

Vaguely she heard him sing something about not being what she needed. Then he stopped dancing and leaned her back against the door of the truck. "But I'm what you need now, aren't I, Julee? I wasn't then. And I won't be later. But I am for now."

Guilt crept in as she accepted the veracity of his words. She was using him. If not for Megan she would never have come back to Blackwood, never have made such an outrageous request. Nor would she ever have slept in Tate's arms again and been shaken by the depth of emotion he could still evoke in her soul.

But no matter how guilty or shaken she felt, there was no turning back. Since their wedding night, she'd been almost embarrassed at how eager she was to be in Tate's arms again. But the truth of the matter remained the same. To make a baby, they needed this element of desire that seemed to burn as brightly now as ten years ago.

Conscious of everywhere their bodies touched, she pulled him closer, stretched up on tiptoe and touched her lips to his.

"Yes," she admitted, heart thudding against the hard muscles of Tate's chest. "I need you."

With a sharp intake of breath he responded, pressing his mouth to hers in a sweet caress.

The surprisingly gentle kiss sent her stomach into a swirling storm of desire.

This was fine. This was good. This powerful pull of attraction would make it easier for her to become pregnant. And once they'd succeeded she would go back to her life in California and Tate could move on with his. They'd made a bargain. And she could not allow herself to fall for him again.

But right now—right now… A soft moan slipped from her as Tate reclaimed her lips, this time with barely controlled hunger. Looping her hands behind his head, Julianna gave herself freely to the rising passion.

The musty smell of oil and dust and the unforgettable scent of Tate McIntyre filled her nostrils. The hard metal of the old pickup dug into her back. When she shifted slightly to remove the pressure, Tate flipped them, effectively switching positions so that she lay cradled in the V of his legs. Immediately, he pulled her down to him, possessing her mouth while his hands possessed her body.

"Mama," a small voice called from somewhere nearby.

Though his eyes were drugged and heavy, Tate snapped to attention in less time than Julianna took to blink. Quickly, he righted her and stepped away. Had she not leaned on the truck, she'd have collapsed.

Megan, followed by the menagerie, came tentatively into the garage, a small frown on her face. "Mama? Where are you guys?"

Chest still heaving, Julianna stepped around the front of the truck and into Megan's line of vision. "We're here, honey."

Coming deeper into the building, Megan squinted up at her mother. "Have you been running?"

At a loss for words Julianna was relieved when Tate stepped forward. "Dancing. Your mom and I used to listen to the radio on this old truck and dance."

"Oh, so that's why you're both out of breath." Hair sticking out from beneath the ball cap, Megan hopped up on the running boards and peeked inside the truck. "Cool. You and Mom drove around in this when you dated in high school?"

Julianna cut a glance at Tate. He was as smooth and cool as lemon sorbet.

"I even took her to the prom in it."

"And now you're married." Megan grinned her heart-stopping smile. "My friend Ashley says it's romantic the way you two got back together after all these years."

Julianna swatted at Megan's bottom. "Ashley's too old for her own good. Now, what do you say we go find some of that lemonade Tate promised us?"

"Okay." Turning on painfully thin legs, Megan led the way out of the garage. "I'm kind of tired anyway."

Julianna tensed, staring at the "angel wings" poking out from the back of her daughter's T-shirt. Certainly the child was weary after the long trip and all the excitement, but the word *tired* served as a reminder that Megan was not a healthy little girl.

"Is she all right?" Tate's voice came from near her ear.

"I don't know the answer to that, Tate." Letting him see the constant worry that plagued her, she looked up. "But if we are very blessed, we'll have a positive answer this time next year."

To her surprise, he dropped an arm over her shoulders and drew her up against his side.

"Then we need to finish what we started back there." His voice lowered to a sexy rasp. "The sooner the better."

A delicious shiver of anticipation, altogether inappropriate considering the temporary nature of their arrangement, danced over Julianna's nerve endings. But appropriate or not, Julianna could hardly wait to be in Tate's arms again.

Chapter Nine

"Is Super Sheriff home?" Megan looked up from her bowl of cereal. "I saw his truck out in the yard."

Taking a glass from the cabinet, Julianna glanced over her shoulder. It was Saturday morning, but Tate's job never ended. "He came in very late and needs to rest as long as he can before the office starts calling him, so please keep the TV down and be quiet."

After three weeks of living with the county sheriff, Julianna never knew what time he'd come stumbling in the door, half-dead. Selfishly, she kept him awake awhile longer until they'd fall into exhausted sleep in each other's arms. By morning, he'd be up and going again.

The town took advantage of him, that was clear, but he let them, believing he owed them that kind of devotion. She'd begun to resent, for his sake, the more senseless intrusions.

"We have a ball game tonight," Megan said around a spoon of cereal. "I was hoping he'd have time to hit me some grounders. I suck at grounders."

Julianna poured herself the usual juice, giving her daughter a wry look. "You do not suck at grounders. You just need practice. If Tate doesn't have time, I'll practice with you."

Megan had been delighted when Tate had asked her to join his Little League team, the Warriors. Between that and her new school Megan had made friends. But most of all she seemed to bask in the extra attention Tate gave her.

"That's okay, Mom. I'll wait for Tate." She pushed the cereal away, then downed the handful of pills Julianna had placed beside her bowl. "Could I take some weenies out for Pitstop? I'm training him."

Taking the empty bowl to the sink, Julianna turned with a smile. The dogs had become Megan's babies. "Training him for what?"

"To come and sit and fetch." She pulled her blue Warriors cap onto her head and confided, "I think he has psychological problems and needs the extra attention."

Laughter bubbled up in Julianna as Megan took two wieners from the fridge, then quietly let herself out the back door. The child was thriving here in the country, and Julianna knew part of the reason was Tate. As busy as he was, he always found time to spend with Megan.

Last Saturday afternoon he'd brought a little boy to the house, his pal in the Big Brothers program, but he'd included Megan in their activities. Together they'd tinkered with the old truck and shot baskets in the pleasant April weather while Julianna had cooked hamburgers on the grill.

Julianna thought of how easily she'd fallen back into the gentle routines of small-town life. She'd joined the health club for the work-out regimen essential to keeping her body in top form. She'd found a church to attend. And she'd even renewed some old acquaintances.

But in the back of her mind lurked the constant worry about finances. She belonged in California. She needed to be there working. What would she and Megan do if her career went south? When her father had died uninsured and in debt, she and her mom had lost everything. She couldn't take the chance of that happening to Megan. But without this chance for Megan to be cured, none of that mattered in the least.

And to add to her concerns, every moment spent with the county sheriff threatened her resolve to keep her heart out of this marriage. Her thoughts went to the gorgeous man sleeping in the other room and a shiver of pure pleasure danced through her.

Outside, she heard Megan talking to the dogs, and from the bedroom came the sound of Tate moving around. Julianna looked at the clock. He'd had all of four hours of sleep.

With a shake of her head, she filled the coffeemaker and pushed the on button. Then she turned to the task of filling Megan's weekly pill planner, carefully counting out the collection of pills that kept Megan alive.

"Morning." The low, gravelly greeting sounded sexy with sleep.

Julianna turned and gave him a smile. "Good morning. You didn't sleep long."

"Long enough."

Already showered and partially dressed, his standard uniform shirt hung open.

Nearly salivating at the sight of his smooth, muscular chest, Julianna turned back to the pill planner. "Coffee's ready."

She heard the clink of the carafe and the gurgle of coffee.

"What are you doing?"

Glancing over her shoulder, she saw him leaning against the counter, his brows knit together in thought. He hadn't been here the other times she'd filled the planner and she could see he was disturbed.

"Preparing Megan's medications for the week." Flipping the plastic lid, she tilted Wednesday's slot toward him, displaying the pills for that one day.

"All those?" he asked in horror. "For one day?"

She shrugged. "You get used to it."

His coffee cup clanked against the counter. "How?"

With a glance downward, she saw the pills as they must appear to him. The truth twisted and turned inside her. Grasping the edge of the counter with both hands, her shoulders slumped.

"That's not true. You never grow accustomed to knowing a handful of pills is all that keeps your daughter alive. You never stop fearing the day when they no longer work or when the cancer returns. Every time I fill this container I thank God for the medication and pray for a miracle. Because that's all we have left, Tate." She tossed back her hair and stared out the window toward the skinny child patiently teaching the bird dog to sit. "That's all we have left."

Usually she didn't let fear gain a foothold, but this morning, with her emotions already on edge over finances and her confused feelings for Tate, the terror pushed to the front, overwhelming her.

Hot tears spilled down Julianna's cheeks and splashed onto the cool white cabinet. Dropping her head, she held back the sobs, refusing to let Tate see her distress. He hadn't signed on for displays of wrenching emotion and she wouldn't subject him to her anguish.

The soft pat of bare feet against tile warned her of his

approach. She sucked in a deep breath, trying to regain control.

A pair of strong arms encircled her from behind, hugging her to his sturdy masculine chest. Compassion, thick and enticing, emanated from him.

"If I could take her illness into my bloodstream, I'd do it," he said softly, his voice intense.

"I love her so much." She began to cry softly.

Gently, holding her like a delicate doll, he rocked her from side to side. "We're going to make her well," he murmured against her ear. "We are. Together."

Julianna drew strength from his persuasive words.

Turning, she slipped her arms around his waist and laid her head on his strong, steady heart. Tate McIntyre was a good man, full of compassion, a man who could never say no to a good cause. For a moment she wished things could be different. That she liked this town. That she wasn't a slave to her lucrative career. And that Tate had married her for love, not altruism. But she knew better than to fantasize about what was happening here. They had a bargain, not a real marriage.

"You must think I'm such a crybaby." She sniffed and tried to pull away with a shaky laugh. "I've cried more in the last few weeks than I have in years."

Refusing to let go, Tate pulled her closer, the scent of his shower soap pleasant, strengthening somehow.

"You're anything but a crybaby." He tilted her face up to meet his green gaze. "You've fought this battle like a lone tigress, but right now you have me. And we're fighting it together." Julianna's heart lurched at the determination in him. "By all that's holy, Julee, we are going to win. Do you hear me? With our help, Megan is going to beat this thing."

To seal his promise, Tate kissed her, his coffee-warmed mouth covering hers in the sweetest caress.

When he drew back with a soft smile, cupping her cheek in the palm of his hand, Julianna felt enormously encouraged.

"You're right. We are going to win. And I don't know how to thank you for giving her this chance."

"She's my daughter, too."

He'd never questioned that, and she loved him for it. In fact, if she wasn't very careful she could love a lot of things about Super Sheriff, as Megan called him. Tate had changed for the better.

"You've turned your life upside down for us."

"The two of you make it easy. Now, come sit down and tell me your plans for today," he said, tugging at her hand.

Julianna knew he was trying to take her mind off her worries and she was grateful, though she yearned to curve back into him and draw from his solid strength a little longer.

She settled into the chair he pulled out. Talking to Tate about the mundane day-to-day activities had become a routine—a dangerously wifely routine.

"Nothing special. Megan wants to swim at the club while I work out and I told Pastor Warick we would help organize donations for the spring bazaars."

"I guess you miss your big church in L.A."

"Certainly," she admitted. "But this one is very… warm, friendly. I like it." A fact that surprised her no end.

She opened the newspaper to the ad section and picked up her scissors.

"What are you doing?"

"Clipping coupons. Here's one for shampoo." She tapped her fingernail against the paper. "A dollar off."

Tate looked at her curiously. "Why are you clipping coupons?"

"A penny saved is a penny earned." She tried to laugh off the implication that someone like her shouldn't worry so much about money.

"You don't need to do that. I can pay for our groceries."

Before she could argue the point, the telephone jangled. Julianna answered.

"Yes. He's here." With a resentful sigh, she tilted the phone toward Tate. He spoke briefly, then hung up.

"Let me guess," she said. "You have to go."

"Yeah." He began buttoning his shirt.

"You're tired, Tate. Can't you stay home and rest one day?" Dear heavens, she sounded like a nagging wife. "I hate seeing you exhausted all the time, and the town never seems to notice."

They expected him to do everything for everybody. Super Sheriff, indeed!

"Not this day. One of the deputies called in sick and the Neighborhood Watch meets at noon."

"And if you miss one civic meeting they'll boot you out of office?"

"Maybe. This is an election year." Downing his coffee, he rose. "Why don't you and Megan have lunch with me?"

Though her brain flashed a warning sign, Julianna couldn't hide her pleasure. "Will you have time?"

"I'll make time. You can go to the meeting with me." He paused, his green eyes roving over her in a manner that made her stomach tingle. "Give me a chance to show you off some more. Not every man in Blackwood, Oklahoma, is married to the prettiest pair of legs in the country.''

Using one of those legs, she kicked out at him playfully, but her question was deadly serious. ''So that's what you think of me, huh? A pair of legs?''

She was fishing and she knew it, the old insecurity rearing its ugly head.

Tate leaned toward her and, in a sexy drawl, replied, ''The rest of the world gets your legs. I get everything else.''

Gripping the chair arms, he leaned down and pecked her on the lips. Then he winked and, with a jaunty stride, headed out the back door.

Stunned and unaccountably pleased, Julianna followed him to the door, then watched the tall, handsome sheriff swing up into his SUV.

The former bad boy with the chip on his shoulder hadn't wanted a wife, but he'd determined to make the best of the situation. And so had she.

The caution light in her brain flashed to red alert.

Julianna stepped out of the bathroom, fresh from her shower. Nervous excitement danced in her stomach. Something else danced in her stomach, too. Something wonderful.

The soft rumble of Tate's gravelly voice came from somewhere in the back of the house. The jitterbug of excitement intensified. After two months of disappointments, she'd waited four extra days to be certain this was no false alarm, but tonight she'd tell him.

She hadn't heard him come in, but then she hadn't expected him this early. It was only nine-fifteen. Though since school had dismissed for the summer, he'd taken to arriving home a little earlier each night, relishing his role as Megan's dad.

Giving a final pull of the comb through her wet hair, she followed the sound to her daughter's room where the sweetest picture awaited her. Tate and Megan propped up side by side on the bed, both dark heads bent over a book. Megan's hand lay trustingly on Tate's shoulder as he read from *Black Beauty*.

Megan looked up with a delighted smile. "Hey, Mama, Super Sheriff is an awesome reader! He does voices and everything."

Tate made a mock swat at the child with the book. "Don't be telling your mother that. She'll expect me to read to her."

Julianna's heart did another jitterbug. In the short time they'd been together, father and daughter had bonded. Tate had taught Megan to shoot lay-ups, to field a baseball and the proper way to plant watermelon. And on those dreaded days when she'd been to the clinic and come home exhausted, he'd patiently sit at the table or in her room and play game after game of rummy or Nintendo. More than once Julianna found them drawing pictures together, and the unexpected burst of happiness staggered her.

"You're so silly." Megan clapped a small hand to her mouth, giggling. "I'm glad you married us. Aren't you, Mama?"

Maybe she *was* glad. And the notion scared her tremendously. She could not fall in love with Tate again. He didn't want that and neither did she. She needed to get back to California, back to work. Megan's astronomical medical bills meant a pressing need for more jobs, not less.

She'd already missed out on an assignment that would have paid well. That was money they needed. And she worried constantly that the agency would tire of waiting for her. If that happened, she had no education, no other skills or resources to fall back on. And then what would happen to Megan? Though Tate expected to help with costs, his salary couldn't come close to covering expenses.

And now with the new baby would come new expenses. Instinctively, her hand went to her stomach. A new baby. She prayed it was true. She wanted this child so much, not just for Megan, but for herself. The anticipation of carrying another child, hers and Tate's, beneath her heart took her breath away.

Tate cut a glance toward Julianna, then back to Megan. "She'd better be glad I married her. Who else would put up with a woman that ugly?" His voice dropped to a stage whisper. "And she snores, too."

Megan squealed with laughter. "She does not! Do you, Mama?"

Julianna managed a smile. When she didn't join in the fun, Tate laid the book aside and sat up. "Something bothering you, Julee?"

She shook her head. "No. Everything is…fine."

Bending, he placed a kiss on Megan's forehead. "Goodnight, Miss America. Time for you and Black Beauty to take a rest."

"Night, Super Sheriff." Megan slithered under the sheet. "Will you teach me that card trick tomorrow? I want to try it on Carly."

Tate tugged the sheet up to her chin. "You bet."

With one last look at his child, Tate clicked off the light and followed Julianna out of the room.

"What's wrong?" he asked abruptly when they'd barely gotten into the living room. "You're not yourself."

"I—" Butterflies moved from her stomach to her throat and threatened to choke her. Would he be as thrilled as she was? Or only relieved that he'd done his duty? Somehow, their lovemaking seemed so much more than duty to Julianna.

Frowning, he gripped her shoulders with both hands. "What is it? Was something wrong with Megan's blood tests last week? Is that it?" Anxiety filled his voice. "Is she sick again?"

"No, no. It's good news." She gave a little laugh. "At least it's the news we've been waiting for."

Tate's strong hands relaxed on her shoulders. Smart and instinctive, he caught her meaning immediately. His face lit up in wonder. "Are you pregnant?"

She nodded. "The home pregnancy test says I am."

The wonder of it, the joy of having another child to love and cherish thrilled her beyond comprehension.

The air buzzed with electricity while Tate absorbed the news.

"Julee," he breathed in stunned awe. "Oh, my God. A baby. We've made a baby." In the next instant, she was picked up and whirled around in a wild dance of pure exultation. "We did it, Julee. We did it."

His laughter was full-hearted and joyous, like a child's on Christmas morning. He reacted as though they were in love, a real married couple who longed for a child together. Julianna allowed herself to bask in the glorious celebration.

When Tate at last eased her back to earth she remained in the circle of his arms, cocooned in the special moment. He cupped her face in his hands, his expression incredibly tender.

"Pretty woman," his mouth whispered over hers. "Beautiful babies."

Then, he did an amazing thing. Tate McIntyre, bad knee and all, swept her up into his arms as easily as he would have Megan, and carried her to their room for the best celebration possible.

*   *   *

Another part of him was lost. If Tate admitted the truth, he'd lost himself entirely this time. There was nothing left that belonged to him. He should feel like an empty shell by now, but he didn't. And that's what scared him most. The more he gave of himself, the more fulfilled he became. Sharing his life with Julee made him whole in a way he'd never experienced. Loving Julee while knowing he couldn't keep her shook him to the core.

Criminy. His chest rose and fell in a sigh of resignation. He loved her, always had. But if she found out, she'd run back to California so fast he'd have to fight to see his children.

His children. Unbelievable joy spread through him warmer than cocoa on a winter's night. He was a daddy, twice over. Children he wanted with all his heart and soul. And a woman he wanted just as much.

Trailing his fingers over the sleeping Julee's silken shoulder, he sighed again. He was in for killer pain. A shudder of foreboding rippled through him. The suffering of ten years ago would be nothing compared to this time.

Chapter Ten

"Feeling better?" Tate gently wiped the perspiration from Julianna's brow.

From the moment she'd cannonballed out of bed and into the bathroom, he'd been here beside her, wet washcloth in hand, waiting for the awful sickness to pass. She hadn't wanted him to see her like this, weak and sick and trembling, but he'd refused to leave.

"It's over." Tilting back her head, she drew in a gulp of cleansing air. "Thank God."

Shakily, she finished rinsing her mouth, pushed away from the sink, and started back toward the bedroom.

"No, you don't." Tate swept her against his naked, sleep-scented chest and carried her to the bed. She lay back against the pillows, sighing in relief.

"We're definitely pregnant," she said with a wry smile.

He stood beside the bed wearing a worried look and little else. "You're pale as a ghost. Are you sure you're all right?"

"I'm fine. In ten minutes or so I'll be terrific."

"Could I bring you some juice or maybe some breakfast?"

She shuddered. "Don't even think about it. Just find me a peppermint."

Tate found the mint, then took a brush from the dresser and climbed onto the bed beside her. He propped his back against the headboard and patted the rumpled white sheets.

"Come over here," he said, making a space for her in the V of his legs. Seeing his intention, pleasure rose in Julianna. Tate could be so sweet. Already feeling less nauseous, she scooted into position, relaxing back against his chest.

With slow, gentle strokes Tate smoothed the awful tangles from her hair, tangles he'd caused last night. The idea of this strong, tough lawman performing such a personal task touched her. He was so tender and solicitous, and she wondered if it was because of the new baby.

"That feels heavenly." And so did he. All the planes and angles of his body molded to her back. She tipped her head back, letting her neck loll in relaxation. The brushing stopped. Tate placed one long, powerful hand carefully over the spot where their baby would grow. Her stomach lifted in joyful response.

"I hope this morning sickness isn't a sign that our boy's going to be a troublemaker like his old man."

Julee smiled. "A boy? I'd like that."

Tate's hand made small circles on her belly. "But another Megan would be good, too."

"I always wanted more kids."

"I always wanted the first one."

"Do you hate me for that? For keeping her from you?" She twisted sideways to look at him. "I didn't do it to hurt you. I meant to tell you, but after you married…"

Her voice trailed off. She couldn't bear rehashing *that* moment.

"I'd have been a lousy father back then, Julee. After I blew out the knee and lost that scholarship I went off the deep end—drinking, fighting, raising all kinds of Cain. Spent more time in Bert Atkins's jail cell than anyone." He gave a short laugh. "Maybe that's why I feel so comfortable as sheriff now."

"All your hopes were pinned on that scholarship." College recruiters and pro scouts had been watching him all through his senior year. Everyone agreed he'd make the big time, and she'd wanted that for him. "You must have been devastated."

"Yeah."

He left it there, hovering between them—fault and blame and loss. The brooding, angry boy had changed so much. Once he'd have raged and stormed against life's injustices, but now he simply worked toward change or accepted. As much as she'd loved him then, he was much more lovable and much more man today. A dangerous, dangerous circumstance to a woman whose primary means of providing for her sick daughter lay fifteen hundred miles away.

For Tate there was no point in mourning the past. Yes, he'd been devastated. Yes, his life had taken a drastic turn. But he'd come out on the other side of the darkness a stronger man and a better one. He regretted not knowing Megan all her life, but he couldn't change that any more than he could change Julee's feelings for him.

There was only one thing he could change—he caressed with great pride the spot where his baby grew—and he'd done that.

Picking up the hairbrush, he resumed brushing Julee's soft hair. It seemed such a small thing to do when she would be the one who suffered sickness and pain to give their child life.

"I'm glad about the baby," he said against her ear.

The kiss Julee placed on the bicep closest to her shot something sweeter than desire through Tate's veins.

"Thank you, Tate. Even though none of this—the marriage, me, Megan, the baby—was in your plans, you've been wonderful about everything."

He didn't dare tell her the truth, that he'd always been a fool for her. And even if he wasn't crazy in love, what had she expected? That he'd turn his back on his own flesh-and-blood daughter, the way his father had turned his back on him?

"We do what we have to in this life, Julee. Some things are just harder than others."

He was thinking of how hard it must have been for her to come to him, to ask him to father another child. And how difficult it was for Megan to live through the hell of chemotherapy and radiation.

She straightened up a little so that their bodies no longer touched. Her voice was quiet, distant all of a sudden. "Speaking of things we have to do. Did I tell you the agency called yesterday?"

The brushing paused. Dread pulled at his insides. He hated when she talked about her work, a constant reminder that Julee was only on loan.

"No."

"They had great news."

"Better than a baby?" he asked.

She rested long fingers on his naked thigh and shook her head. The motion released the subtle fragrance of her hair.

"Not even close. But a really exciting campaign is in the works and I'm up for it."

In these months of living with a model he'd learned enough lingo to know that a campaign was a big deal, a chance to exclusively represent a company or a new product.

"You mean, after the baby comes?"

"That's the great news. This is for now, when I need to be working so badly. The agency recommended me because they knew I was trying to get pregnant and the campaign includes maternity wear. I'd have to go to L.A. for a few weeks, but now that I'm pregnant that won't be a problem. And here's the best part." She swiveled around to face him, blue eyes dancing. "If I get an exclusive endorsement, they want all of me, not just my legs."

Tate's hand slid down the side of her silken hair, caught the tips just over her breast and held on. For two months he'd pretended she was really his, but now the career she'd chosen over him once before would win again. He heard the excitement in her voice and knew she would leave. Heck, she was already gone.

"I've always wanted to be more than a parts model, Tate. And this is one of the biggest designers in Hollywood. A campaign with his company will pay enormously and the TV residuals could go on for a very long time. They're even talking about a commercial during the Super Bowl! Can you imagine the money that will bring in?"

He knew she worried over finances. Had heard her on the phone with her accountant. Had watched her gnaw on a pencil as she pored over bank statements and medical bills. As sheriff he pulled in a decent income, but his check couldn't compare to the amount Julee was accustomed to. If this job would make her happier, more secure, he wanted her to have it. But he didn't have to like it.

He breathed in her sweet, clean scent and held it in his nostrils. His insides felt like lead. She'd never stay with the likes of him anyway. Might as well accept the inevitable.

"When are you leaving?"

"I'm not. Not yet anyway. The agency has sent in my portfolio, and if the designer decides I'm the model for the job, I'll ask Mom to come back here and help with Megan. Then I'll go."

"So the deal isn't settled?" The hope made him guilty.

"No. They might not decide for a while, but I've worked a long time for an opportunity like this. I want this contract, Tate. I want it so badly."

A squeezing pain gripped Tate's heart. He'd given her a baby, but still she wanted more. What could that no-account McIntyre boy and the provincial little town of Blackwood have to offer Julianna Reynolds? No glamorous job. No huge contract. All he had was himself. And that had never been enough for anyone.

"If this is what you want, I'm glad."

"Thank you." The corners of her lush mouth lifted. "If I can only win the contract, everything will be perfect."

Perfect wasn't the word he wanted to use.

He cupped her upturned chin, tried to smile and failed. Resigned, he kissed her gently on the forehead, then laid the hairbrush aside and eased off the bed.

"I guess I'll get ready for work, then. If you're all right, I mean."

"I'm fine, Tate, really." With a soft smile, she reached out to run her fingers lightly over his naked chest. "Sure you don't want to be a few minutes late for work this morning? Celebrate our double good news some more?"

Goose bumps the size of marbles prickled his skin. Even now, when she'd rejected him again in favor of her career, he wanted to please her. For weeks he'd despised his weakness because he couldn't stay away from her. All he could think about was getting home to Julee, talking to her and listening to her laugh, reminiscing about old times and sharing new ones, watching her tool around in his kitchen as if she'd always be there as his wife. He'd let his job suffer and he'd alienated some important people to arrive home at a decent hour each night, but these few months with his family were worth anything.

And now that she had what she needed, she was leaving him again. This time she might not come back at all. If he had an ounce of self-preservation left, he had to stop acting like one of his stray dogs, begging for affection.

Swallowing back his own cry of protest, he rose from the bed and said, "Maybe we shouldn't."

"Shouldn't?" She sat amidst the rumpled sheets, blue eyes wide and puzzled. "Why not?"

Tate crammed a hand over the top of his head to keep from reaching out to her. "Look, Julee, we've done what we had to. You're pregnant. Maybe that should be the end of it."

Her stunned expression said she understood what he was suggesting. "Do you mean you don't want us to—"

"Right. I don't want us to," he lied.

Unable to bear her baffled, pained expression, and fearing he'd fall on his crippled knee and beg her to stay forever, he turned away and began to dress.

All that day, Julianna vacillated between hurt and anger at Tate's announcement. During her workout at the gym. While Madeen repaired the nail she'd destroyed planting pansies. Even when dear Mrs. Barkley had offered to teach Megan to play the piano, she'd hardly been able to show her gratitude.

Now, as she drove up the graveled road toward Tate's

place after dropping Megan off at a friend's house, the humiliation lingered like the smell of fried fish.

Tate had left her that morning, kneeling on the bed like a beggar while he yanked on his clothes and bolted out the door.

His words of cold reality had splashed over her like ice water. He was a man of duty. Hadn't she seen that in every weary task he completed as sheriff of this town? He'd had to make a baby with her for Megan's sake, and now that he had, he didn't want to touch her again.

Well, what had she expected? None of this had been his idea. She'd come back into his life, laying guilt on him. Otherwise he would never have wanted her here. Hadn't he made that clear during the bone-marrow drive?

That was fine. Really. She had no room in her life for love and a real marriage even if Tate had offered. She had a duty to continue her lucrative career as long as possible. And if she was awarded the new ad campaign, everything would be fine.

Then why had she curled into a ball, one hand protecting her precious new cargo while she cried into the pillow that still carried Tate's warm and wonderful scent? And why had she been sick inside all day long?

With self-disgust, she slammed the heel of her hand against the steering wheel.

Dust churned behind her as she made the final curve toward home past the occasional illuminated farmhouse. A coyote loped across the road in front of her headlights and disappeared into the trees.

She was later than she'd intended, but Carly's mother had been a classmate in high school, and they'd reminisced awhile.

As she pulled into the driveway she saw that Tate had beaten her home, an unheard-of event. Jitters began dancing in her stomach. What would she say to him? How would he act?

Clicking the locks on the car, Julianna crossed the yard and strode into the house, posture stiff. She'd be cool and polite and pretend he was a friend, not a lover.

But the minute she saw him all her resolve flew out the window. Still dressed in uniform he limped around the kitchen holding on to a chair as he scooped ice from the freezer into a plastic bag. His teeth were bared in an expression of excruciating pain that tore at her heart. The television must have drowned out her entrance because when he glanced up and saw her there, he quickly masked his suffering.

"Hey," he said, a little too breathlessly, Julianna thought.

"Hey yourself. What happened?" She dropped her purse on the nearest chair and went to him, not caring one whit that he'd rejected her only twelve hours ago. "Go sit down."

"I can do it."

"Do what I said, Sheriff."

Taking the bag from his hand, she finished scooping the ice, and noted with relief that he'd started toward the living room. He made it as far as the doorway, then grunted and grabbed for the jamb. Sweat beaded his forehead.

"Crap!"

Julianna rushed to his side and shoved her shoulder beneath his armpit. "Come on, tough guy. Lean on me."

He resisted. "You're pregnant. I'll hurt you."

Warmth suffused her at his protectiveness.

"Baby and I are made of strong stuff. Now, either lean on me or I'll kick you in the kneecap."

He managed a weak grin. "You're a mean woman, Julee."

But he relented, letting her assist him to the couch. With her help, he swung his legs up, then collapsed into the cushions, face pale, teeth clenched.

"I'm all right." He reached for the ice.

Ignoring him, Julianna placed the bag on his knee. Even through his jeans the joint looked swollen.

"That looks bad. Let's get you out of these pants."

"Ah. A beautiful woman wants to take off my clothes and I'm in too much pain to enjoy it."

Julianna gave him a sharp look. Considering what he'd said this morning, his attempted joke hurt more than it amused.

He unbuckled his belt and Julianna helped him slide the jeans downward. They stuck at the top of his boots.

"This may hurt." She took his booted foot into her lap.

"Got a bullet I can bite on?" He grabbed for his knee, bracing it between his hands.

"You're the sheriff. Get your own bullet." She gave a steady pull and, grimacing in remorse when his laugh turned to a groan, removed the boot.

The second boot as well as the jeans came away much easier, though droplets of sweat beaded Tate's forehead.

"I'm sorry about that," she said. "I'll get a towel to go under the ice pack. Would you like some aspirin or something?"

"Yeah. There's a prescription bottle in my sock drawer."

Surprised, she turned to look back at him. In all the time they'd been together he'd never taken so much as an aspirin. He shrugged sheepishly and Julianna knew admitting he needed pain medication hurt his pride.

After finding the pills, she gathered a towel and a glass of sweet tea, taking them all to him.

"Are these pretty strong?" She handed him the white caplet.

"Yeah. Doc told me only to take them when the pain was really bad."

Julianna glanced inside the bottle dated three months earlier. "Have you taken any at all?"

"One."

"Stubborn mule."

"You know how I feel about drugs and alcohol."

"Medication is not the same thing." But she knew his worry. His mother was addicted to both, and after his own brief battle with drinking, he was taking no chances. The knowledge squeezed at her heart. The tough lawman would rather suffer than succumb to the deadly weakness.

"Let me look at that knee."

"What do you think you can do for it, doc?"

Playfully, she swatted his shoulder. "Just let me look." She lifted the ice pack and gasped. "Good heavens, Tate, this is swollen to twice the size of the other one. What did you do?"

"Rough day at the office."

"I'll say." She eased down on the couch beside him, staring at the injury. "What did you do? Smart off to Rita the Magnificent?"

"I overdid it. That's all." He reached down and massaged the thigh muscle directly above his kneecap.

His reluctance to discuss the injury piqued Julianna's curiosity, but she didn't press for information. She was far too concerned about his pain.

"Here," she said, replacing his hand with hers. "Let me."

Gently kneading the muscular flesh, Julianna's gaze was drawn to the road map of scars dissecting his leg. One scar the shape of a fish skeleton stretched from groin to knee.

Another sliced down the side of his calf, and still more zigzagged across the kneecap.

"Such a catastrophic injury," she murmured, compassion and a sad sickness welling in her as she considered all he'd suffered because of this knee.

"I'll be all right by morning."

She traced the scars with the tip of her finger. Looking at them had always hurt too much and had kept her from asking about the ugly details. But now she had to know. "No, I mean the first time. When you were hurt playing football."

"Oh."

"Tell me about it. This looks like more than one surgery."

"Two. The other scars are where the kneecap came through the skin."

"Dear Lord." She closed her eyes against the horror of it, but her imagination saw him lying on that football field, writhing in agony while she paraded her long perfect limbs in front of a camera.

Aching with regret, she compared her shorts-clad legs to his. Hers smooth and pale and pampered. His dark and muscular and covered with these horrific scars. With little forethought, she bent and placed her lips on the swollen flesh crisscrossing his kneecap.

Tate's sharp intake of breath drew her gaze upward.

"Why'd you do that?"

"Because I wasn't here to do it ten years ago," she answered softly, then kissed him again and again.

"Ah, Julee." He squeezed his eyes shut, sighing heavily. When he opened them, a sad surrender emanated from the green depths. "Come up here."

A ridiculous hope flared. "But this morning you said…"

"Can't I just hold you?" he interrupted, and the quiver of disappointment embarrassed her.

Tugging, Tate pulled her upward. Careful not to bump his knee, she wedged her legs between his and lay atop his long, wide body. His big hands stroked her hair away from her face. Then he drew her down to his chest and wrapped his arms around her.

Through his shirt Julianna felt the strong steady beat of his heart against her cheek. The faded scents of starch and woodsy cologne combined with the heated fragrance of Tate's skin. The hard contours of his body molded to hers so perfectly. To her confusion and dismay, she wanted to snuggle into him, to absorb him for those future times when she'd lie in her condo alone.

They remained that way for the longest time while Julianna pondered Tate's odd behavior. This morning, he'd practically thrown her out of his bed. Now, tonight, he was holding her. She had meant to comfort him, but somehow she felt comforted.

Julianna raised her head. "How do you do that?"

"Do what?" The words rumbled in his chest.

"Make me feel better when you're the one hurting."

"Ah, Julee. You don't get it, do you?" His tender smile was tinged with an emotion she couldn't identify.

"No. I don't think I do."

"Let me show you." Taking her face in his hands, he kissed her forehead, then stared into her eyes for several beats. While she waited, puzzled, pulse racing, he moved his mouth over hers in a kiss so heartbreakingly intimate that she couldn't miss his meaning. He wanted her.

Bad enough not to understand her own feelings, but Tate seemed as confused as she.

She drew back, breathless and more perplexed than ever. "But what about this morning? You said—"

His answer was deep and husky. "I lied."

Then he kissed her again.

Much later, after they'd stumbled and limped into the bedroom, Julianna replaced the melted ice bag with a fresh one, then propped on one elbow beside the reclining Tate and draped an arm across his chest.

"Are you going to tell me what happened to your knee?"

Careful not to disturb the ice pack, Tate shifted toward her. He blew out a long, ragged breath. "I caught Melton Scott and his chop-shop ring red-handed. Needless to say, they weren't too happy to see me."

Suddenly Julianna comprehended what she'd seen earlier. Tate's dirty shirt, his scratched arms, and the bruise that dotted his left cheekbone.

"They're the ones you've been after for months, aren't they? Did they try to escape?"

"We had a little scuffle. Melton went straight for the knees."

Anger ripped through Julianna. "Why that—I hope he's in jail."

Tate shook his head, his worry obvious. "There's the problem. Half the people in town refuse to believe that a man with Melton's clout and wealth would be involved in anything illegal. Suddenly I'm the bad guy instead of him."

"Because you arrested him?"

"Yeah." He swiped a hand down his face. "He'll make bail by midnight."

"Are you in any danger?" she asked, alarmed.

"Not the kind you mean." He cupped her chin. "But my career as sheriff in this county could be in jeopardy."

"That's ridiculous!"

"No, darlin'. That's politics." His thumb caressed her cheek, offering comfort when he was the one in need. "Melton is a rich man with more friends than Pitstop has fleas."

Julianna saw his concern. He loved being sheriff, but he would always do what was right even if it wasn't popular. "You work too hard. And they don't appreciate you enough."

"Yeah, well, don't worry about me. You've got a new baby to think about now." He snugged her up against his side. "After you and Megan go back to California I'll have plenty of time for mending fences."

There was the crux of Tate's problem. Compelled to be the perfect father and husband interfered with his ability to remain the perfect sheriff. As soon as she and Megan were out of his hair, he could get his career—and his life— back on track.

Chapter Eleven

Slamming out of the SUV on a perfect autumn evening Tate followed the aroma of grilled chicken into the back-yard and tried to push the worries over his campaign into the background. Soon enough Julee would read the ugly allegations against him in today's newspaper. No use bringing trouble to the dinner table.

Wearing a white chef's apron over her pregnant bulge, Julee waved a spatula and smiled. "I hope you're hungry."

He pumped his eyebrows and gave her a wolfish once-over. "Starved."

As the months had passed and she'd begun showing, Tate had grown more fascinated than ever by her body. He'd heard that a woman was increasingly beautiful and sexy during pregnancy, but he'd never noticed the difference in other women. He did with Julee and was filled with awe to know he'd had a part in those changes.

"I thought we'd eat out here on the patio since the

weather's so pleasant.'' She motioned to a round table set with a blue tablecloth and yellow mums.

"Great.'' He bent to kiss her, a habit he'd grown to enjoy as much as the pretty feminine touches around the house. Dangerous, perhaps, but he'd come to accept the good with the bad, grasping the pleasure while it lasted. One thing for sure, coming home eased the stress of his job in a way it never had before no matter how bad the campaign was going. "Where's Megan?''

"Inside. Will you tell her to come on out and eat?''

"You bet.''

In minutes, he and Megan returned and the three sat down to dinner.

"Chicken, rice, corn on the cob. Mmm,'' Tate said, as he piled his plate high. He'd never expected her to cook for him, never expected a lot of the things she'd done. If he didn't know better, he'd think she actually enjoyed being here.

"And chocolate cake for dessert.''

"Dessert?'' She seldom fixed dessert, calling sweets wasted calories. "What are we celebrating?''

He forked a bite of chicken and nearly moaned over the delicious savory herbs. Lunch had been a drive-through burrito.

"The agency called today.''

His stomach went south. Suddenly the chicken wasn't quite as tasty. "Your modeling agency?''

Julee nodded, face aglow with excitement. "They want me for the ad campaign.''

His lousy day just got lousier. Months had passed since she'd first mentioned the campaign. Very carefully, he lifted his napkin and wiped his fingers. He'd known this moment would come, dreaded it on the best of days, but the timing couldn't be worse. "Congratulations.''

Her smile faltered. "I thought you'd be happy?"

Happy? Hardly. She was carrying his baby, and he wanted to experience every moment that he'd missed with Megan. He wanted Julee, too, but he didn't dare admit that little secret. She'd been more than clear about the temporary aspect of their marital arrangement.

"You need to rest, not be standing on your feet all day in front of a camera."

Julee glanced at Megan. "Honey, would you go inside and bring out that chocolate cake now?"

Megan glanced from Julee to Tate, then shrugged. "Okay. Ice cream, too?" she asked hopefully.

"Sure."

When the child was out of hearing range, Julee said, "I haven't worked in months, Tate. Do you have any idea how expensive a stem-cell transplant will be? Or how long Megan will be on maintenance care afterward?"

"I'm not exactly broke, you know." Not yet anyway. "I have some investments and if worse came to worst, I could sell my land and take on another job. There are ways, Julee." He wanted to beg her, to get down on his crippled knee and plead with her not to leave him again. "Work with me on this. Give me a chance to take care of you and Megan. I can do it."

Over a plate of salad and chicken, she stared at him with the strangest expression. He could swear she wanted to believe him.

Feeling a surge of confidence, he played what he considered his ace. "Think about this, Julee. Megan can't go to L.A. She has school and her medical team is here. Who will look after her if you leave?"

For some reason the light in Julee's eyes dissipated and her shoulders drooped. "Yes. For Megan. You're right of course," she said dully. "As I mentioned before, Mom will come and stay with the two of you while I'm gone."

There was the truth, much as it pained him. Whether love or money, what he had to offer was never enough. Julee didn't want to be here. She belonged in L.A. with her rich and successful friends. He felt like one of his stray dogs, groveling for affection.

Megan, toting the cake and ice cream on a tray, returned then. She must have sensed the tension between the adults because she frowned from one to the other as she slid into her chair. "Are you two fighting?"

"Of course not." No way he'd upset Megan. This was his problem, not hers—or even Julee's. She'd never intended to stay. "Your mother was telling me about the great new job offer she has. She's going back to California for a while."

"I don't have to go, do I? Carly might get to have a party at Halloween." Eyes worried, she chomped down on an ear of corn.

"I'm afraid you're stuck with me and your grandma."

"Grandma's coming?" She glanced at Julee. "When?"

Julee reached over and wiped a buttery kernel from Megan's cheek. "In a couple of weeks."

More disappointment filtered through Tate. "But the election is only three weeks away."

She laid a hand on his. "I'm sorry. I wanted to be here."

His chest hurt so badly he thought he'd explode. He was about to lose his job and now he was losing the woman he loved all over again. He fought back a wave of bitterness. He hadn't meant to love her, hadn't meant to let her under his skin again. He'd always known she planned to go back, but that didn't keep his heart from shattering into a million pieces.

* * *

During the next week concern over Tate's campaign continued to grow, and that concern pushed the modeling job to the back of Julianna's mind. She'd been inexplicably disheartened that Tate hadn't minded if she left as long as Megan remained, but seeing Tate hurt over this election bothered her more.

First, a smear tactic funded by friends of Melton Scott. Then, the resurrection and rehashing of Tate's less-than-stellar youth. And last of all, the rumors that he ran a corrupt office.

For Julianna the festering boil came to a head Wednesday afternoon at the local supermarket. She stood with one hand on the creamed corn—Tate's favorite—and the other on her aching back when she heard the sheriff's name coming from somewhere beyond the black-eyed peas.

"You know why the sheriff is out to get Melton, don't you?"

"Something to do with Julianna Reynolds is what I heard."

"You heard right. When the three of them were in high school, Tate was always jealous of Melton's money and position. The two of 'em got in a fight once because Julee and Melton had eyes for each other. Been bad blood between them ever since."

Shock ricocheted inside Julianna like a bullet in a metal room. She remembered that fight. One night after a dance, a very drunk Melton had tried to force Julee into his car. Tate still bore that tiny scar on his face where Melton had hit him with a beer bottle. And she recalled Melton's vicious taunts about Tate's parentage and her own morals. Then, as now, Melton Scott had been a spoiled brat, determined to have his own way no matter who got hurt.

Angry enough to open a can with her teeth, Julianna left the store without buying a thing. After all Tate had done for this town, yet human nature wanted to believe the worst about him. They all needed a good reminding of how hard he worked, of how much of himself he poured into the Little League, the senior citizens, the school, and every other social program in the county. They needed to remember the criminals he'd pulled off the streets and the times he'd endangered his own life to make Seminole County a safe place for them to live.

He'd given up so much for her as well as this town. She'd asked everything of him, and he'd asked nothing but that she give his children his name. And what did he get as repayment? The prospect of losing the job he loved so much. Surely there was a way for her to help now that he was in need. But how? What could a leg model possibly have to offer a political campaign?

Shaking so hard she could barely get the car key in the lock, she slid into the seat and slammed the door. She wasn't good at much, but she could throw a party. And that's exactly what she would do. Blackwood was about to experience an old-fashioned, band-playing, speech-making political rally.

From sunup to sundown for the next week a steely-minded Julianna pounded the pavement, recruiting volunteers and cajoling donations from every merchant and business in the county. Just as she'd organized the bone-marrow drive with stunning efficiency, she whipped together a campaign attack worthy of a professional.

Soon the reality of what she was doing hit her. There was no way she could stop now when Tate needed her so badly. She fought it, worrying about finances and anxious to work, but in the end the desire to help Tate won out. If she hoped to turn the tide in this election, going to L.A. was out of the question. She couldn't stay here forever, but she could do this.

Slick, polished ads appeared in the paper, on the radio and local television. Posters created by Megan and her school friends went up all over town. Most of all, Julianna talked. She talked and smiled and charmed, using her pregnancy and her celebrity to every advantage. Her homecoming remained big news and she used that, appearing on local talk shows and news programs to garner free publicity that Tate's opponents would have to pay for. She had never felt so successful in her life.

When the night of the big party arrived—a barbecue held at the city park—the crowd flowed in, dragging lawn chairs to set up around the perimeter of the huge concrete pavilion. To Tate's surprised satisfaction, even members of the opposition party appeared, either curious to see what would happen or too greedy to pass up the free food.

In the perfect October Indian summer evening, the mouth-watering aroma of barbecue wafted up from a smoker the size of an oil tanker. Tense, but more than pleased, Tate stood beside Julee on the back of a flat-bed trailer, which had been pulled alongside the pavilion to serve as a stage. Behind them a country band tuned up, twanging guitar strings to a perfect pitch with an electric piano.

"Look at this crowd, Julee. How did you do it?" He was amazed at her organizational skills.

She waved off his gratitude. "Oh, it was nothing."

"Nothing? What are you talking about, woman?" He leaned away and studied her beautiful face. She had no idea of how talented she was. "Twice this year I've watched you whip this county into a frenzy in support of your cause. You could do this for a living."

Stunned blue eyes met his. "You're kidding, right?"

She looked adorably kissable in a short lime-green overall, the bulge of his baby around her middle downright sexy. He loved looking at her. And after what she'd done for him and his campaign, he danged near worshipped her.

"I'm not kidding. You're a natural at this. I know a dozen politicians that would give their eyeteeth for someone with your skills and ability to generate interest and excitement."

"Anyone could do what I did."

"No, sweetheart, they couldn't." He slid an arm around her, the tips of his fingers brushing her belly. Even at five and a half months she wasn't very big, but big enough that she tired easily. And for the past two weeks she'd flown around like a migrating hummingbird.

"Shouldn't you go home now and rest our baby awhile?"

"And miss all the fun?" Her laughter glided across his nerve endings like satin sheets. "Not a chance, Sheriff. I feel great and so does baby McIntyre. Tonight this town is going to sit up and take notice, and I wouldn't miss that for the world." She pointed toward Megan and a group of her friends coming toward the platform. "Here we go."

She pulled him down into the lawn chairs set up toward the back of the trailer where they could see everything. And everyone could see them.

A lump the size of a Dodge truck parked in Tate's chest. Waving mini pom-poms and dressed in their Warrior T-shirts, Megan and a half dozen other fourth-graders jumped onto the stage and chanted:

McIntyre for Sheriff. McIntyre's the one.
If you don't vote for McIntyre, you're no fun!

The cheer went on for several embarrassingly sweet verses. Then, amidst cheers and clapping, the girls pranced off the stage. When Megan stopped to blow a kiss his direction, his heart filled with a love so powerful he could hardly contain it.

So began the process of speakers, a mishmash of everyday citizens willing to speak up for that McIntyre boy from the wrong side of the tracks; just plain folks, each with a brief story to tell about the sheriff who'd been there when they needed him. Holding Julee's hand in a death grip, Tate looked on in humble amazement.

All the while his mind chanted the name of the woman who'd brought all this to pass. Julee. Champion of the underdog. Wonder worker of organization. What did it mean? Why had she gone to so much trouble to help him?

The last speaker rose from her lawn chair and with a rickety gait started toward the platform. Rising, Tate moved forward to assist the tiny, withered lady.

Georgia Barkley saw him coming and wagged her cane at him. "I can make it, boy. Git back over there with that pretty wife of yours. She's pregnant, you know," she declared, stating the obvious with such relish that everyone laughed.

"Now." She wobbled up to the microphone where Tate stubbornly waited to lend a hand if needed. "All of you people know me. I taught half of you to read back in my teaching days. And it's a crying shame you're using that skill to spread this nonsense about our sheriff. Don't you people know how hard this man's worked?" She pointed out a walrus-faced man near the front. "Angus Fleming. Your filling station stays open until midnight, doesn't it?"

At the command in Mrs. Barkley's school-teacher voice, Angus sat up straight. "Yes, ma'am. Seven days a week."

"How many nights has the sheriff come by to check on you before closing?"

"About every single night, I reckon."

"And you, Heck Jones." A bony finger picked out her next student. "When you're out on the garbage truck at 4:00 a.m. do you ever see Sheriff McIntyre?"

"Sure do. Lights are on in his office most of the time."

"You see what I'm getting at? His office is open all day and he spends time with your kids in the evenings, then works most of the night." She nailed the crowd with an accusing stare. "We run this boy ragged. I don't know when he sleeps. Shoot, I can't even imagine when he had time to make that baby."

The crowd roared with laughter. Tate grinned over at Julee whose cheeks blossomed bright pink. He gave her a naughty wink.

"Don't get me wrong." Leaning heavily on her cane, Mrs. Barkley went on in her thready voice. "I'm as guilty as the rest. He's made many a trip to my place to look for a Peeping Tom. Why, who'd peep at an old bag like me? But he came anyway. Now, if we don't keep our Sheriff McIntyre in his office, who's going to take care of these things? And who's going to bring Penelope her cat food? I'll tell you who." She banged her cane against the wooden platform. "Nobody."

Affection for the lonely widow bloomed as Tate realized how long it had been since she'd called him. Not once since Julee had hired her to teach Megan piano. He missed that.

"So," Mrs. Barkley continued, "it's time we nipped all these silly lies about him right in the butt."

Suppressing a laugh, Tate leaned down and corrected gently, "In the bud, Mrs. Barkley."

"There, too. And some of you folks need more than a nip. You need a swift kick for even thinking our fine sheriff would do anything underhanded." To nods and smiles, she said, "Now, this isn't a funeral, you know. It's a celebration to honor the finest sheriff we've ever had. I got a little song I want to play." Tottering toward the electric keyboard set up to her right, she asked the pianist, "Mind if I borrow your pee-ano?"

Grinning, the keyboard player relinquished his seat. Georgia Barkley sat, then ran a few tentative chords. She leaned into the microphone. "I haven't ever played one of these electric pee-anos, so here goes nothing." The PA system squealed and she jerked back. "Lord o' mercy."

Tate didn't know what to expect. But Georgia Barkley ripped into a Scott Joplin ragtime tune with a stern admonition that everyone dance, and the park erupted. People spilled out of their folding chairs and bee-bopped onto the concrete pavilion.

Tate laughed out loud and grabbed Julee by the wrist. "You heard the lady. Let's dance."

They zigzagged around the platform for the duration of Mrs. Barkley's tune, but when she turned the music back to the band a slow dance began, Tate pulled his breathless wife toward him.

"You've put me in a dancing mood, Mrs. McIntyre." He bent for a kiss, lingering long enough to make him wish they were home alone.

"Good. You needed a little fun and relaxation." She slid her arms around him and rested her head against his shoulder. "How's your knee holding up?"

"Fine." The heck with his aching knee. He nuzzled her ear. "I don't know what to say, or how to thank you for this," he murmured, his voice growing gruff with emotion while all around them people danced and talked and ate barbecue. "I feel...I feel..." He couldn't find the words.

"Shh. I know." Julee pressed soft fingertips to his lips. "People just needed a reminder, Tate."

But he knew what she'd done. She'd made him realize

for the first time that this town not only respected him as a lawman, they cared about him as a person. She had no idea what that did for a man who'd grown up the mixed-breed bastard of a shady woman, always the outcast.

He pulled her to him, to hold her close in gratitude and love. "You've done so much."

She smiled. "You ain't seen nothing yet, Sheriff. We still have lots more work to do between now and election day."

"But you're leaving on Tuesday."

She laid a long-nailed hand against his cheek. "Some things are more important than money, Tate. After all you've done, I couldn't leave you to fight this alone."

He stepped back, puzzled. What was she saying? "The designer campaign—it's what you always wanted. Aren't you going to L.A.?"

"I canceled the trip, turned down the contract. There will be other ad campaigns. Elections only come every four years."

Blood pounded in Tate's temples and he was certain his bad knee was about to give way. Julee had turned down the assignment of a lifetime for him? What did it mean? That he was more than a sperm donor? That she trusted him to provide for her and Megan?

Settling his chin on her head, he breathed in the smoky essence of her hair, loving her so much he ached. And for the first time in many years the boy from the wrong side of the blanket felt loved in return. Julee, the woman who'd shattered his life, was giving it back to him.

"Julee," he pledged, "I'll find a way to take care of us. We'll be all right."

She touched his cheek. "Of course we will."

Bitterness, long buried inside him like a festering thorn, lifted and floated away on the scent of barbecued ribs.

He grabbed her hand and squeezed it against his chest, unable to stop the words that tumbled out. "I love you, Julee. I've always loved you."

Julee heard the sweet words but didn't reply. Instead she laid her head against his chest and remembered the last time he'd said them—ten years ago before she'd stepped on that Greyhound bus. And as soon as she was out of sight, he'd found another woman. Would he do the same the next time she left for L.A.? Even if she wanted to believe that he loved her, the memory of that betrayal wouldn't go away.

Julee worked tirelessly on Tate's campaign during the next weeks and when at last the victory came, she was delirious with excitement. Tate, too, was overjoyed and seemed lighter, happier, more comfortable in his own skin. The town's affirmation, she was certain, had done that for him.

Thanksgiving came and then Christmas. They celebrated in small-town style with a parade down Main Street and Megan's school play in the auditorium. All the while the need to work pressed on Julee's mind as hard as the baby pressed on her heart. She'd missed her opportunity to model while pregnant, so all she could do now was bide her time until after the delivery. Funny how every moment spent with Tate made her that much more reluctant to return to L.A. But return she must. Her life was there and so was her livelihood. She belonged in California just as Tate belonged here. They had made a bargain and she would keep her end of it.

Chapter Twelve

Julianna awoke to the terrifying sound of retching. Terrifying because it wasn't her own. At eight months she was long past morning sickness.

The cold January morning added to the chill up her backbone as she rushed into the bathroom to find Megan violently ill.

"Mama!" the shaking child managed.

Stilling her own trembling, Julianna lightly laid a hand on her daughter's feverish face.

"What's wrong?" Tate's voice, husky from sleep, rumbled from the doorway. Out most of the night, and operating on fewer than three hours' sleep, he came instantly alert at the sight of Megan. Clad in plaid flannel lounge pants and a T-shirt, his presence armed her with a strength she didn't know she had.

"I'm not sure. We need to get her to the hospital."

Tate disappeared and reappeared fully dressed in an unbelievably short time, carrying with him a flannel blanket.

He said, "Tell me when she can travel. I'll have her in Oklahoma City in thirty minutes or less."

"I have to get dressed."

"Go. I'll take care of her."

Seeing the intent set of Tate's jaw, Julianna hurried out of the room. He would take on the devil and win to protect his little girl.

"Tate." Megan's small voice quivered as she reached for him. She never called him Tate. Julianna's fear shot up a notch.

As quickly as possible, given the advanced state of her pregnancy, Julianna yanked on black tights, a black turtleneck, and a red corduroy jumper, all the while listening to Tate soothe their sick, frightened child. By the time she returned to the bathroom, Megan was wrapped in the blanket and cradled in Tate's strong arms.

"Ready, Miss America?" Though his smile must have been forced, it elicited a feeble grin from Megan.

With uncanny skill and speed only a cop could get away with, Tate delivered them to the ER in considerably less than the promised thirty minutes. Because Julianna had been on the cell phone most of the way, the doctor had been notified and the nurses immediately whisked Megan away.

As their child disappeared into an examining room, Tate draped an arm around Julianna's shoulders. "You okay?"

Numbly, she shook her head. "No. Are you?"

Drawing in a deep breath, he pulled her against his chest in a gentle hug and rested his face in her hair. "Maybe it's just a virus."

The buttons on his shirt rubbed her cheek as she nodded, drawing comfort from his stalwart strength. "This time of year schools are full of sickness."

His hand made circles on her back. "Do you think we messed up by letting her attend public school?"

"No," Julianna said adamantly, pulling back. "Remember how proud she was of her part in the Christmas program? After the transplant she'll have to be separated from people for weeks, maybe months. She needed this time to be a normal kid."

A door swooshed open and a tiny woman wearing a white lab jacket and an oversized pair of glasses bustled out. Tate and Julianna went to meet her.

"Dr. Knight, how is she? What's happening?" Julianna battled to keep the panic from her voice. Tate's hand kneaded the nape of her neck, sending a message of reassurance.

"We're running some tests." The doctor patted Julianna's arm. "Don't be overly concerned just yet. This could be a reaction to the medication or even a twenty-four hour virus."

"That's what Tate said."

Dr. Knight nodded toward the tall sheriff who towered nearly a foot over her. "Why don't one of you go up on the floor and help Megan get settled while the other takes care of the paperwork in the admitting office? I'll be up to talk with you as soon as I have a better idea of what's going on."

"I'll go with Megan," Tate said. "Julee, you know more about her information than I do."

Julianna agreed, walking as far as the elevators with Megan and Tate where she kissed her daughter's forehead and winked. "Be up in a minute, sweetie."

When Julianna arrived a short time later, a wan Megan lay nestled among the pristine sheets, an IV dripping into one arm. No matter how many times she'd repeated this scene, Julianna hated it, wanting to cry out at the injustice of a child suffering so much.

Her heart lurched at the sight of Tate, chair drawn up to the bed, head bowed in an attitude of prayer, holding Megan's small hand between his own huge ones.

Gratitude and love swamped her. She needed him so badly. Many times she'd faced Megan's illness with only her mother's support, but somehow everything was different with Tate. It was as though his very presence could thwart the ugly cancer.

She barely whispered into the room, but Tate heard. Still clinging to Megan's hand, he stood, moved to one side, and offered Julianna his chair. Gingerly, she eased into it, supporting her basketball middle with one hand.

"They gave her something for the nausea." He stood quietly behind her right shoulder. "The nurse said it would make her sleepy."

Megan opened heavy-lidded eyes to whisper. "I'm better. Don't worry."

"You'll be up and out of here in no time." Tate smoothed the dark hair away from Megan's face as her eyes fluttered closed again.

Tate's prediction proved untrue.

Later that morning, Dr. Knight reappeared along with Julianna's obstetrician and the stem-cell specialist. The moment she saw the three of them together tears welled in Julee's eyes. This could not be good news. His hand holding hers, Tate escorted her into the waiting area.

Dr. Knight's brown eyes were compassionate behind the wide glasses. "Preliminary blood work shows some early blasts." She glanced at Tate's questioning frown. "Blasts are abnormal white cells that indicate the leukemia's return. Nothing we can't handle, but a sign that we need to begin the total body irradiation and set a date to induce labor.''

Overcome with the terrible possibility of harming one child to help the other, Julianna covered her belly protectively. ''It's too early.''

''Another ten days' time, after a round of tests and Megan's radiation treatments, will put you close to thirty-eight weeks. That's perfectly acceptable gestation. Dr. Travis,'' the tiny oncologist said, nodding toward Julianna's obstetrician, ''wants to perform an ultrasound today. Then we can make the final decisions about an induction date for you and the transplant date for Megan.''

After months of planning with this team of top-notch physicians, Julianna knew what was supposed to happen. Megan would undergo radiation treatments to kill every hiding cancer cell, eradicating her immune system in the process. For the last portion of the treatment and for weeks afterward she'd be in isolation, shielded from the germs and the company of everyone except her parents and her medical team. Meanwhile, Julianna's labor would be induced and the baby safely delivered. Finally, Dr. Franks would harvest the healthy stem cells from the umbilical cord and infuse them into Megan in a procedure much like a blood transfusion. If all went well, Megan's bone marrow would multiply the new cells and she would be free of cancer forever.

But now that the time had come Julianna was panic-stricken. She looked to Tate. ''We've come so far, and we're so close to the end of Megan's nightmare. But I want this baby, too. I love him, Tate. We can't let anything happen to him.''

''Nothing will happen to our baby.'' Jaw set, he glanced toward the closed door of Megan's room. ''Neither of them.''

With all her heart, Julianna prayed that Tate was right.

* * *

Nine days later Julee stood at the cash register inside Harper's Doughnut Shop. This was the first time she'd left Megan's side since the radiation had begun, but she'd made a quick trip home for clean clothes and the new baby's homecoming outfit. Even now, with her mother and Tate at the hospital, she felt the need to rush.

The baby inside her stirred. Lovingly, she caressed the mound with her hand. Tomorrow was his birthday. It was also Valentine's Day, and Megan loved the bakery's cherry heart pastries. Maybe she couldn't eat them, but she'd have them.

The rich warm scents of cinnamon and fresh bread swirled around her head. The doughnut shop, endearing in its small-town flavor, baked from scratch every morning the recipes brought to America from Czechoslovakia by Clare Harper's grandparents. And nobody made better fruit-filled pastries.

"Hello, Julee." Clare, round face glowing from the kitchen heat, sported a bright-red polyester pantsuit in honor of the holiday. The pants stretched tight across a backside that carried an extra doughnut on each side. "How's your little girl?"

"Pretty well, considering." In a hurry to get back to the city, Julee avoided a detailed explanation. "I want to take her some of those cherry hearts she loves so much."

"Oh, honey." Clare looked crestfallen. "We sold the last ones about ten minutes ago. But I have the dough already made—not that frozen stuff they use at the other place—and I can bake up a fresh batch in ten minutes flat."

"I'm in a bit of a hurry, Clare."

The baker's gaze dropped to Julianna's middle. "You're not in labor, are you?"

"No, no. I just need to get back to the hospital."

"Eight minutes, Julee, and I'll have that child a special treat. Sit down and take a load off." She bustled toward the kitchen, calling over her shoulder. "Eight minutes, I promise. I'm just sick not to have those ready for you. And that sweet child wanting them. Oh, I'm just sick about it."

The tension of having to wait added to the uncomfortable puffiness of her feet, so Julee sat down at one of the wrought-iron tables. She'd swear nothing in this bakery had changed in ten years. On the back wall hung a hand-lettered list of prices. And above the non-computerized cash register was a sign that read, If you don't believe in the resurrection of the dead, come back at closing time.

Julee smiled at the small-town warmth and humor. As she gazed about, trying to keep her mind off tomorrow and all it would mean, a small blond woman stepped in from the blustery outside. Julee's stomach dipped. In the months in Blackwood she'd managed to avoid Tate's ex-wife, but this winter's day her luck had run out. She swallowed back the bitterness that rose at this living reminder of Tate's betrayal.

Clare's shiny face poked around the kitchen entrance. "Oh, hi, Shelly. I got that sweetheart cake fixed up for Larry just like always." She winked. "You romantic fools you. I'll have Kathy bring it out in just a minute." She looked in Julee's direction. "Six minutes, Julee."

Clare's words turned the newcomer's attention toward Julee. Tate's ex-wife came across the room, eyes kind in a gentle face. "How's your little girl doing? I heard she's back in the hospital."

Julee gave her stock answer. "Pretty well, considering."

How did you tell people that you were scared out of your mind that this could be the last week or month of your child's life?

"Is the transplant still on for tomorrow?"

Ah, the joys of living in a small town where everyone knew your business almost before you did.

"Yes, tomorrow." A tiny foot poked at her rib cage.

"And the baby, too, I understand." Shelly pulled out a chair and sat down uninvited.

"Yes." Julee twisted the ring on her finger and wished Clare would hurry.

"Tate must be delirious about the new baby. He's crazy about kids."

Julee shifted uncomfortably. "Uh, yes." The last thing she wanted was a conversation with this woman about Tate.

"Julee…" Shelly hesitated, a small frown between her eyes. "I hope I'm not making you uncomfortable."

"No. No. Of course not." Julee forced a laugh. Where were those cherry hearts?

"Good. You have no reason to feel threatened by me. Tate is my friend. That's all he's ever been."

A friend? Now that was interesting. Aloud she said, "I understand."

Shelly didn't look convinced. "Has Tate talked to you about us? About what happened back then?"

Julee sucked in a breath of warm, yeasty air, at a loss for words. Really. The last thing she needed today was to rehash Tate's betrayal of ten years ago.

"I can see he hasn't." Kind brown eyes regarded her. "I'm not surprised. That was a terrible time for him."

"The football scholarship meant so much to him."

Shelly gave her a funny look. "But do you know why he wanted so badly to succeed in football?"

Oh, she knew all right. "It was his ticket out of this town."

"It was his ticket to L.A., the way he planned to get you back. By playing pro ball he would have something to offer you so you would come home."

"Maybe at first, but—" She waved a manicured hand in the air, the solitaire twinkling in the artificial light.

"But he married me? Is that what you're thinking?" Shelly twisted the strap on her purse. "Tate's a good man, and he'll never tell you this out of kindness to me and my family. But if I were you I'd want to know."

"Really, Shelly. This is not my business. Tate and I—" She hesitated, having almost admitted the ugly truth. That she and Tate were only a temporary arrangement. After tomorrow, the marriage would be over. "All that's in the past."

"The past is the father of the present. Everything we do affects someone else. I learned that the hard way ten years ago. Tate was the town bad boy, always in trouble, and I was one of the few people who knew why. I'd always had a crush on him, bet you didn't know that."

Julee shook her head. She hadn't. She'd been so wrapped up in herself during those high-school days she'd paid no mind to an underclassman.

"Tate thought he'd lost everything—his college education, his chance to play pro ball, and most of all you. We got together because I'd listen to him talk about you. And he was so grateful and needed someone so desperately, he married me when I asked."

Julee glanced up at Shelly's wry smile.

"Yes. I asked him. Talked him into it after only a couple of weeks together. I was young and foolish and romantic. I thought I could fix him. He was very wounded, a tortured soul who thought he would never be good enough for you without a football career. Did you know he hated that people were so hung up about your legs and your looks? You were so much more than that to him.''

Numbly, Julee shook her head. Tate had actually said that?

''Don't get me wrong. I wasn't a martyr. I was crazy about him in a mixed-up, juvenile kind of way. But after a couple of years I grew up. By then he had quit drinking and getting into trouble, trying his darnedest to repay daddy and me. But we had married for all the wrong reasons. Tate tried. Oh, he tried so hard, but we both knew what a terrible mistake we'd made. I always knew he loved you. Because no matter how hard he tried in the daytime, he couldn't stop having those dreams.''

Julee blinked. ''Dreams?''

''In his sleep, the truth came out. He would call your name.'' Shelly's voice dropped to a near whisper. ''And sometimes he cried.''

Julee squeezed her eyes shut against the searing image. Tate. Oh, Tate, what did we do? How could I have been so blind?

Shelly's words were like a sledgehammer banging away at the years of bitter resentment. She'd thought she was the only one who had shed tears. But all the time she'd been lost and lonely in an unfamiliar city, grieving for him, Tate had loved her, longed for her, and nearly killed himself with grief.

The truth came then, freeing her from ten years of pain. She loved Tate McIntyre, had always loved him. That's why she'd turned down the best modeling job of her career. Because Tate had always made her feel like more than a pair of legs. He made her feel loved.

She opened her eyes and suddenly the world around her had changed. The scales fell away, and she saw what she'd missed ten years ago when she'd been desperate to leave Blackwood. All that time in the plastic modeling business, she'd felt alone. Fighting Megan's cancer, she'd felt alone. Coming back to Blackwood, she'd felt alone.

But she hadn't been. The people in this little town with their bad polyester and their nosiness had always been here, caring. The shallowness, the emptiness had been inside her. She had become a snob of the worst kind by not giving credit to the good and decent people who had always cared. Plain, unglamorous people who did the best they knew how. People who'd donated blood and stood up for Tate. People like Clare who'd busted her tail to make cherry hearts for a sick child. And like Shelly, a sweet ordinary woman who'd cared enough to bare her past mistakes to a virtual stranger.

And most of all Tate, who'd always been here, loving her, waiting for her to come home.

Clare bustled out from the kitchen all smiles, carrying a white box. "Here you go, Julee. I fixed 'em special. On the house."

Tears clouded Julee's grateful eyes as Clare flipped open the box. Inside lay six golden hearts, still warm and fragrant, each emblazoned with a red, frosted *M*.

She'd run all the way to California searching for success, chasing a dream when all the while everything she needed had been waiting right here. The dear, sweet people of this town had been waiting. And so was the man she loved.

Valentine's Day dawned cold and overcast. Excited, nervous, scared out of his mind, Tate hadn't slept fifteen minutes the night before. His life would take a dramatic change today. His son would come into the world—for indeed, the ultrasound promised a boy. Megan would have her new chance at life. And in gaining these two miracles Tate would lose the only family he'd ever known. He tried not to think of the joy and pain he'd experience this day, but in truth, he could think of little else.

As his boots thudded down the tiled hospital hall, Tate considered how in less than two weeks this pediatric ward had changed him forever. As a police officer, he'd seen much of human tragedy, but nothing compared to the loss that resounded within these walls. Loss of innocence. Loss of life. This was a place of life and death, of healing and suffering, of hope and despair, all mixed together and difficult to distinguish. And the valiant spirit of the children here, eking out every moment of joy and love, moved him as nothing ever had. Now he understood fully Julee's commitment to the cause of increasing the number of bone-marrow donors.

Tate's mouth lifted as he entered Megan's isolation cubicle, his yellow paper gown rustling. Julee and her mom, who'd flown in as soon as she'd heard the news, had decorated the walls of Megan's room for Valentine's Day. Hand-drawn Valentine cards made by Megan's classmates, pictures, balloons, heart-shaped lights, and get-well banners covered the walls and doors and brought cheer into the tiny, crowded unit.

"Hey, Miss America. Looking good."

In truth, Megan was as bald as a cue ball and black circles rimmed both eyes. But true to her unquenchable spirit she'd polished her head with blueberry glitter gel. "Hi, Super Sheriff. How's Mom?"

Tate sat on the bed, one hip connecting with his daughter's. "Great. She's down on the second floor right now, getting everything set up. Sometime this afternoon, you will be a big sister. Then, later tonight, Dr. Franks will do your transplant. And before you know it, you'll be out playing baseball again.''

''Yeah.'' Falling quiet, she picked at the tail of her hospital-issue gown. ''Tate…''

When she called him Tate, he knew she was serious. ''What, darlin'?''

''I didn't want to ask Mama about this, because she worries too much. And with the baby and all…'' Her voice trailed off while she mustered up the courage to say whatever was on her mind. When she did, the words came out in a rushed whisper.

''What if I die?''

Tate's heart set up a wild bongo beat, squeezing off his air. For all her outward show of optimism, his baby girl was afraid. At the age of nine, a time when her young mind couldn't even comprehend what was happening, Megan was forced to face the possibility of death. She had a right to be scared. He certainly was.

''You won't.'' He couldn't bear to acknowledge the possibility.

''But what if I do?'' Anxious green eyes beseeched him. ''Nathan did.''

Three nights ago, while Tate and Julee encouraged a tired and frightened Megan, an eight-year-old had lost his battle with leukemia. Shocked and grieved, they'd listened to the family, crying outside the room. The event had had a profound effect on all of them, making the threat of death a very real possibility.

What could he say? How did he promise her something that wasn't in his control?

''I know I'll go to heaven,'' Megan went on in her small voice. ''But I'd rather stay here with you and Mom and the baby. There're still so many things I want to do.''

The lump in Tate's throat threatened his breathing.

"Like what?" Maybe if he got her talking, he could take her mind off her fears.

"Oh, you know." Her hands fluttered in the air. "I want to be a teenager. Drive a car. Go out on dates. Stuff like that."

"Drive a car!" Tate's pretend shudder drew a smile from Megan. "Now there's a scary thought. And dates! Whew, I don't know about that. I'd have to buy a BB gun to keep all those boys away."

Megan giggled. "You wouldn't do that."

"Just wait and see," he teased. "Why, they'll be lining up on the front porch wanting to take you to the prom and I'll pick them off one by one." He squinted over his cocked finger.

Megan batted his hand away. "Silly, I won't ever get to go to a prom."

Sweet baby. Was she afraid she'd never live that long? "Why not?"

She gave him a look that said he didn't know a thing. "Because I can't dance."

Weak from relief, Tate stifled a laugh. Dancing he could deal with.

"Sure you can. Come here." Mindful of her IV, he swooped her off the bed. She weighed next to nothing. "Stand on my boots."

Face aglow with fun, she placed both narrow bare feet atop his and trustingly lifted her arms. He took her hands, placed one on his shoulder and held the other. Smelling of antibiotic and blueberry glitter gel, the top of her head barely reaching the hollow of his chest, she felt as fragile as a baby bird. He yearned to crush her to him, to imprint her smile, her effervescence, her sweet, loving spirit forever on his memory. Instead, he held her lightly and forced a smile.

Humming "I Will Always Love You," he waltzed her gently around the room, bad knee throbbing and heart aching with love as the IV pole rattled along beside them like a third partner. He wouldn't be there for her prom, but he was here now and he could give her this.

After a minute or two, she stepped off his boots, breathless, face flushed. "Could we rest now?"

"You bet." Contrite at tiring her radiation-exhausted body, he returned her to the bed and sat down, angling toward her. "You're a great dancer. A regular prom queen."

She grinned. "Will you teach me more later?"

Again, the need to be upbeat outweighed the need for honesty. He wouldn't be around to teach her anything. "You bet."

"I made something for you." From the bedside table she retrieved a red paper heart and handed it to him. "It's your Valentine."

Leaning back into the pillow, a watchful Megan waited for him to open the card. Her thin hands picked at the neck of her gown.

The moment he read the inscription, which ran uphill and was written in childish cursive, Tate struggled to keep the smile on his face and the mood upbeat. What he really wanted to do was weep with joy and love and loss.

Dear Super Sheriff. Sometimes I pretend that you're my real dad. I wish you were. I love you. Megan.

"Do you like it?"

Closing the card, he held it thoughtfully between his palms. "I love it. I love you, too."

She nodded matter-of-factly. "I know. I can tell. You love Mama, too."

"Yes, I do," he answered honestly, his voice thick with unspoken emotion.

"I'm glad. We love you, too. Before you married us, Mama was all stressed out. Since we moved here she laughs a lot and she acts happy, especially when you're at home. And she's not so worried all the time. I mean, until I got sick again this time. I know she's worried about me now. And the new baby. I hate it when she worries."

Tate's insides did a flip-flop. Could Megan be right? Was Julee really happier here than she'd been in L.A.? Last night she'd come back from Blackwood pensive, thoughtful and saying little. He knew she worried about today, but could she also be dreading the end of their time together?

He glanced at his watch, the copper band reflecting the fluorescent lights. "Speaking of your mom, I need to get back down there. They should be starting her labor anytime now. Need anything before I go?"

She shook her head. "Will you come back and tell me as soon as the baby comes?"

"You bet. And later, after she's rested awhile, I'll bring your mom up." He rose, slowly straightening his knee.

"Cool. Where's Grandma?" She and her IV rattled along with him to the doorway.

"With your mom. But she'll come up and stay with you as soon as I get down there." Gripping her face between his hands, he placed a kiss atop her blueberry-glittered bald head, relished her responding giggle, and left the cubicle.

Outside, he removed the yellow gown and crumpled it into the wastebasket. A nurse, carrying a tray of medications, gowned and entered the room.

As he started to leave, a pecking sound turned Tate around. Framed by Valentine hearts, Megan appeared in the small observation window that connected her to the ever-watchful eyes at the nurses' station. She held up a walkie-talkie, the hospital's ingenious method of allowing contact with friends who couldn't go inside.

Attached to the wall next to the window was the twin radio. Tate lifted it from its holder and pressed the button.

"Miss me already?" he teased.

She smiled, a fleeting hint of sunshine that turned serious. "If something bad happens to me—"

So he hadn't allayed her fears. "It won't."

She persisted. "But if it does, will you take care of my mom? She'll be real sad, but don't let her stay sad too long."

"Megan—" How did he explain the complicated actions of two adults to a child who might not see tomorrow? Helpless, Tate searched for the right words.

"Promise," Megan insisted, green gaze earnest as she raised a hand to the window and placed it on the glass between two paper hearts. His child, courageous and strong in a way he couldn't begin to comprehend, waited for his pledge.

He thought of the piano music those fingers had yet to play, the drawings they had yet to create and so much else she had yet to experience. And still, her concern was for others.

His gaze flickered to the nurse behind Megan. Their eyes caught, held. Above the V-shaped ridge of the yellow isolation mask, the woman's eyes glistened with tears.

An answering set of tears burned behind Tate's eyelids. He placed his palm against the window, eclipsing Megan's much smaller one. The promise wasn't his to make, but the love pulsing through the glass could not be denied, and Tate could no more refuse than he could rise and fly. "I promise."

Somehow. Some way. He would not let her down.

All his life, he'd been on the outside, nose pressed

against the pane, yearning for the warmth and love within. But this little girl and her mama had welcomed him inside. And the sweet glory of belonging had taken a broken man and made him whole.

His throat ached and his chest threatened to explode.

This was his daughter. They were his family. Heaven above, he would do anything to keep them. Megan loved him. And though, out of fear and self-preservation, he'd been blind to all the signs, Julee loved him, too. He was certain of it. Everything she said, everything she did pointed to her love. Maybe he'd never be good enough for her. Maybe he didn't deserve her. But he could love her like nobody else ever had or ever would.

He'd made a promise to this little girl, and he would keep it. No matter the consequences. No matter the cost. Even if he had to give up the job he loved and move to the city he despised, he wouldn't let Julee go this time without a fight.

Tugging the IV pole alongside her, Julianna hiked the tail of the annoyingly revealing hospital gown and scooted onto the bed. The nurse readjusted her monitors and left the room.

Last night she'd returned from Blackwood deep in thought, trying to come to grips with the revelations in Harper's Doughnut Shop. Then while Tate had slept in the chair beside Megan, she had stared down at his beloved face and made a promise.

She hadn't yet worked out the details, but she could no longer live an empty life, pursuing only fame and fortune. Talking to Shelly had taught her an important lesson. She'd put her trust in her job, in money, even when she had plenty. But it had been love—hers and Tate's—that had been needed to save Megan's life. And that love, not her career, would see them through the hard days ahead.

She loved Tate McIntyre with every fiber of her being and this time she was certain he loved her, too. She couldn't wait to tell him.

The basketball masquerading as Tate's baby executed a particularly fine lay-up and her belly responded by undulating madly. She was laughing when the door swooshed open and Tate stormed in. Her heart did a perfect imitation of her belly.

Looking intense, he approached the bed like a man on a mission. "I changed my mind. I can't do this."

"Excuse me?" An IV tube was taped to the back of her hand and a pump beeped and clicked, injecting the medication to begin her labor. Beside the bed, a monitor amplified the flub-flub of the baby's heartbeat, whirring out an occasional strip of paper covered with incomprehensible squiggles. Julianna gave them all a wave of her hand. "I'm hooked to every machine known to medical science. The pitocin drip is started and any minute now contractions strong enough to bring down an elephant will start. I'm sorry, Sheriff, but changing your mind is not an option."

"That's not what I've changed my mind about."

"Thank heaven." She smiled up at him, feeling happy and free in a way she didn't fully comprehend. Making the right decision did that for a person. "How's Megan?"

"Good." He shoved a hand over the top of his spiky hair, then shook his head. "No, that's not true. She's scared. You know what she asked me?"

"What?" Her chest tightened. Or was that her tummy? She laid a hand upon the latter.

"She asked me if I'd take care of you and the baby if something happened to her. She doesn't want you to be sad."

"Oh." Tears sprang to her eyes. She pressed a hand to her lips. "Oh, my sweet, precious little girl."

"I promised her, Julee. And I keep my promises." He looked ready to fight about something.

"Okaaay." Not sure where he was coming from or where he was headed, she waited.

"I said I'd give you a divorce after the baby came, but I won't. I can't. Megan's going to get well."

"I believe that with all my heart." Though, again, she had no idea what Megan getting well had to do with the divorce.

"And she needs her father. She needs me." He stomped to one end of the room, then stomped back to the bed. "I have to shoot the boys off the front porch. Who else can do that?"

With the monitor beeping and her tummy squeezing Julianna had a hard time following. "Tate, what are you talking about?"

"You, me, Megan, the baby. We're a family. Families need each other. I never knew that, never had that, but now that I have it I'm not about to let it go."

Mind whirling, Julianna tried to make sense of Tate's disjointed tirade. A twinge of discomfort low in her belly made her squirm, but she kept her attention riveted on Tate. Something was happening here and by heaven, she wasn't going to miss it.

"Me, neither."

"No, don't argue." Lost in his one-sided debate he paced back and forth missing the giggle that slipped from her lips. "If you want to live in California, then I'll live there, too. Whatever it takes. Whatever I have to do. I'll be your gardener, your chauffeur, your baby-sitter. Heck, they're bound to need cops in a place that big."

Suddenly everything became clear. Like the moment

a cloud passes and the sun comes out, full and bright. "You'd live in L.A.?"

"If that's what you want."

"I don't."

"Maybe I'll never make enough money, but I'll bust my butt trying. I'll drive a cab. I'll bus tables. I'll even hang from the side of one of those blasted skyscrapers and wash windows." He shuddered at the thought.

A hiccoughing giggle stopped his tirade. "Tate, didn't you hear me? I don't want to live in L.A. anymore."

He stopped pacing and blinked at her, bewildered. "You don't?"

"No." How did she explain that six cherry hearts and his sweet ex-wife had opened her blinded eyes?

"Then what do you want?"

"Knowing you'd give up the job you love and follow me to L.A. is so special, but I don't want that. I want to raise our kids in Blackwood—together—where we both belong. I love you, Sheriff McIntyre."

He dropped his head back and spoke to the ceiling. "Thank God. I've loved you all my life, Julianna. All I ever wanted was to make you happy."

"It took me so long to understand that. All those years ago, when I called to tell you about Megan only to discover you had a wife, I thought you had never loved me at all."

"That wasn't true—not then, not ever."

"I know that now. I was missing you. You were missing me. And neither of us had the self-confidence to trust the other."

"If only we'd known in time about Megan, I never would have…" His green eyes clouded with regret. "That was a bad time for me."

"I know. I talked to Shelly yesterday."

His face softened with the knowledge of what she knew about him. "Even when I tried to drown the truth in a bottle, Shelly always knew I loved you. She's a good woman."

"A very good woman. Just as Blackwood is a wonderful town."

Bending over the bed, he kissed her softly, then rested his forehead against hers. "I thought you hated Blackwood."

"That was a long time ago, Tate. Oh, I'll admit I never planned to come back, but when I did the town drew me in like a warm fire on a freezing night. And Megan has blossomed there in the country sunshine with so many caring people around her. I didn't realize how tired and lonely and stressed I was until I rested awhile in my hometown and was loved by the finest man I've ever known."

"What about your career?" Ever mindful of the tubes and cables running from the bed, Tate sat down on the bed beside her. "You've worked hard to be a success, and if a modeling career is what you want then I want it for you."

"It isn't. Not completely. I like my work, but nothing is as important as you and our children. Being without a job scares me, but being without you terrifies me."

"Then why can't you have both? You can jet off to L.A. for occasional jobs while I hold down the fort. You'd be home more than you'd be away. We can make it work if we try hard enough."

"You mean, commute to L.A. and work part-time?"

"Sure, why not?"

"Well, I—" A smile erupted inside her. "Yes, why not?" Julianna reached her hand out to him, clasping his warm, callused palm in hers. "See? You're doing it again."

"Doing what?" He leaned close, almost lying down in

the bed with her. Her skin tingled deliciously where his warm breath brushed her cheek.

"Making me feel better." She located the tiny scar on his jaw and traced it, remembering the boy who'd taken abuse for her sake. The same man who'd willingly turned his whole world upside down to give their daughter a miracle. "You're so good to me, Tate. I love you."

"Do you? Are you sure?" He moved close, his mouth hovering over hers. "Will you marry me, Julee? I mean, marry me forever?"

She pressed her fingers against his mouth, stopping the oncoming kiss. "Oh, yes, I certainly will. If you promise to always love me."

With a growl, he nipped at her hand. "Lady, I've loved you all my life. I loved you as an angry, messed-up teenager and I loved you for the ten years you were gone. But on this day, with our little girl upstairs waiting on her miracle, and our baby son about to be born, I love you even more."

He yanked her hand away and captured her lips with his. She responded with a moan, totally inappropriate considering the slam-dunk her basketball had just made.

He pulled back, grinning his sexy grin. "I take that as a yes."

"Absolutely, positively, yes." Suddenly a deep, grabbing pain pinched her eyes into slits. "Ooooh. Wait." She grappled for his hand and then for her belly. "I think we'll have to finish this conversation later. Right now—oh, shoot. Right now, your son is playing one-on-one with my insides."

"My son," he said in stupefied wonder. "Criminy, Julee. We're having a baby."

And there on Valentine's Day, between murmuring encouragements and shouting I love you's, that's exactly what they did.

Epilogue

"Mom. I'm open. Throw it to me."

Arms waving frantically, fourteen-year-old Megan galloped coltlike toward a space between two lilac bushes, otherwise known as the end zone.

In an all-out sprint, football tucked against her side, Julianna glanced behind her. Her pulse rate, already in overdrive, shot up another notch. Tate and his partner, five-year-old Nathaniel, bore down upon her like two raging bulls, one with a pronounced limp and the other on chubby, baby legs. Both wore identical expressions—determination and glee.

With a squealing laugh, Julianna let the football fly, then raced toward her daughter, trying her level best to block the two oncoming McIntyre males.

"Touchdown!" Megan shouted, thrusting the ball high overhead. Then, in a crazy celebration dance, she wobbled her knees and spiked the ball between her legs. Julianna arrived and the ladies jumped skyward in a fancy high-five. "We finally did it! We won!"

Tate and Nathaniel loped up beside them.

"Pretty good catch, Miss America."

"Thanks, Dad." Megan slapped him a high-five. "I had a great coach."

Julianna treasured the besotted expression that crossed Tate's face every time his daughter called him Dad. Megan had been overjoyed to discover that the man she already loved was her real father.

"How about another game?"

"Yeah," Nathaniel said, chubby hands on his knees in imitation of his father. "We want 'venge."

"That's *re*venge, squirt," Megan said, tossing him the ball.

"Vengeance will have to be deferred to a later date, guys." Julianna patted her heaving chest. "I'm beat."

"Awww." Nathaniel's full lower lip protruded in disappointment. Big blue eyes batted up at them. Julianna held back the laugh. Her baby boy, as darkly handsome as his father, already knew the power of his male charm.

"Hey, squirt. Come on." Megan looped a comradely arm over the much shorter child's shoulders. "The two of us can play something." Green eyes twinkling toward her parents, she bent low and whispered loudly. "Old people have to rest a lot."

"Yeah. Old people have to rest a lot." The boy perked up. "Will you push me on my bicycle?"

Nathaniel was learning to ride without training wheels. For the last three days, Megan had served as his official safety net, running alongside him with one hand on the back of the seat while his short legs pumped madly.

"Sure. Race you to the porch." And off they went, Megan's long, athletic legs holding back, while her little brother ran with tight-fisted determination. At the last minute, Megan sprinted alongside him, making it a race to the finish, but letting him win in the end.

The two adults crossed the sunlit yard much more slowly, hands entwined. A hummingbird whirred overhead, then darted toward a crimson hibiscus.

"Where do they get all that energy?" Breathless, Julianna plopped down onto the shaded front steps and shoved back the hair pulling loose from her ponytail.

Tate landed beside her, flopping backward to lie on the cool concrete. Sweat rings circled the underarms of his tank top. "Wherever they get it, it's a wonderful thing."

"Yes, it is, Sheriff. Who would have thought five years ago that we'd have two gorgeous, healthy kids running around in our backyard?" For indeed, Megan had passed her five-year checkup with flying colors and had been pronounced "cured" of the deadly leukemia.

"Who'd have thought we'd even have a backyard—together?"

Her heart lifted in pure wonder at the amazing changes the last five years had brought. "No kidding."

The newest stray dog ambled up and shoved in for some attention. Absently, Julee gave his ears a rub. "Mom called today."

"How're they doing?" Beverly and Eugene had married two weeks after Julianna had announced her intention to remain in Blackwood.

"Eugene's retiring next month. They're buying a Winnebago."

"Get out of here."

She laughed. "They want to travel. See the country. They'll come through here and leave an extra key to the house for me to use whenever I'm there." She'd long since sold the condo and had Eugene invest the profits, staying with Beverly and Eugene on her occasional trips into L.A. "Which won't be too often now."

"I like this Dallas thing." Tate propped up on one elbow and trailed his fingers over her bare calf. "Do you?"

She'd recently switched to an agency in Dallas where she could do more catalog modeling. The money wasn't as good, but the drive to Dallas from Blackwood was short enough that she could come home every night. Now that Megan was well, the need for large contracts no longer pressed, but the need to be in Blackwood with her family did. Tate had been right when he'd insisted they would make it somehow.

"Yes, I do. Working out of Dallas leaves me more time for you guys and to work on my new job." The pleasure of accomplishment warmed her. With Tate's help and encouragement, she'd begun working part-time as campaign organizer for several political candidates, a job she relished.

"You know something, McIntyre? Life is just about perfect. Thanks to you."

He sat up then, looped an arm around her neck and pulled her to him. "Nope. All the thanks go to you. My life was an empty, workaholic shell before you stormed into Blackwood demanding my blood and my baby."

"You still work too hard." Though he organized his work much better to allow for family, Tate remained the adored sheriff, giving of his time and energy to Seminole County.

"Yeah, but I'm not empty anymore. You fill me up, Julee. Those kids fill me up. I never knew I could be so happy."

Julee stroked his bristled cheek. Love and joy and thankfulness welled inside her. "Oh, my sweet, sweet husband. You have no idea how you complete me. How you helped me believe in skills I didn't even realize I had. How you made me secure when I was so afraid. And of course, our babies. Our precious, beautiful babies.'' She sighed. ''We should have had a dozen.''

''What do you mean should have?'' Tate brought his face in line with hers, green eyes dancing mischievously. ''I'll give you all the babies you want, woman. Just say when.''

Pleasure warmed her. She'd been thinking about it a lot lately. ''So, you're willing to make another baby with me, huh?''

A gleam she'd come to love leaped into his green, green eyes. A responding excitement stirred in her veins.

''Willing.''

He gave his eyebrows two sexy pumps.

''Ready.''

Playfully, he body-slammed her onto the concrete porch.

''And very able.'' He kissed her.

Her laughter disappeared inside Tate's warm, loving mouth. The fire, so easily ignited, flamed to life.

''Mommy. Daddy. Look!'' Nathaniel's excited cry jolted them both upright.

''Hold that thought.'' Tate laughed wryly, then gave her one last promising kiss. ''Unless I miss my guess, some monumental event has just transpired in our son's life.''

''He's riding by himself.'' Megan trotted alongside the bicycle, hands off. ''It's a miracle.''

''Yes, a miracle.'' *And so are you.* Julianna watched, heart full. *Both of you.* She slid an arm around her husband's waist and rested her head upon his heart. *All of you.*

For indeed, Megan's miracle had become a miracle for them all.

* * * * *

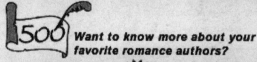

COMING NEXT MONTH

#1710 MAJOR DADDY—Cara Colter

When five adorable, rambunctious children arrived on reclusive
Cole Standen's doorstep, his much needed R and R was thrown
into upheaval. But just when things were back to the way he
liked them (ie. under his control!), Brooke Callan, assistant to the
children's famous mother, arrived. Could Brooke and the brood
of miniature matchmakers rescue this hero's wounded heart?

#1711 DYLAN'S LAST DARE—Patricia Thayer

The Texas Brotherhood

Pregnant physical therapist Brenna Farren was not going to let
her newest patient, handsome injured bull rider Dylan Gentry,
give up on his recovery *or* talk her into entering a marriage of
convenience with him! But soon she found herself in front of a
judge exchanging I dos—and getting a whole different kind of
"physical therapy" from her heartthrob husband!

#1712 AN HEIRESS ON HIS DOORSTEP—
Teresa Southwick

If Wishes Were…

Jordan Bishop fantasized about being a princess and living in
a palace. But when her secret birthday wish was answered
with…*a kidnapping,* she was rescued by the sexiest innocent
bystander she'd ever seen. She found herself in his castle—
and in the middle of a *big* misunderstanding! Could the love-
wary Texas oil baron who saved the day be Jordan's prince?

#1713 THE SECRET PRINCESS—Elizabeth Harbison

The princess was alive! And she was none other than small-
town bookstore owner Amy Scott. Despite her protests, Crown
Prince Wilhelm insisted the skeptical American beauty return
to Lufthania with him. But while Amy was sampling the royal
lifestyle, Wil found himself wanting to sample Amy's sweet kiss-
es.…